FIORELLA DE MARIA

The Vanishing Woman

A Father Gabriel Mystery

IGNATIUS PRESS   SAN FRANCISCO

Cover images:
Photograph of woman © iStockPhoto.com
Photograph of tree by Vincent Chin on Unsplash.com

Cover design by John Herreid

© 2018 Ignatius Press, San Francisco
All rights reserved
ISBN 978-1-62164-223-7
Library of Congress Control Number 2017951077
Printed in the United States of America ∞

THE VANISHING WOMAN

I

Gabriel took a deep breath, rather like a swimmer about to plunge into icy water, before he stepped from the warmth of the presbytery into the bitter cold of the courtyard. Even with the protection of a thick black coat, he felt the chill of that early December evening and pulled his hat down firmly over his ears. For once, he was grateful for the long black woollen scarf Mrs Whitehead had knitted for his birthday the previous month and wondered whether he could prevail upon her to knit him a pair of matching gloves for Christmas if he asked her very nicely.

The presbytery sat snugly next to the Church of Saint Patrick, a building ludicrously out of character with the rest of the street, with its large, garish green doors complete with shamrock door handles, but he had become quite fond of the old place in the nearly three months he had ministered there. The priest who had built the church some fifty years before had been an Irish member of the Salesians of Don Bosco and had made no secret of his political allegiances. The bars protecting the street-side windows were an unfortunate reminder of the attack on the church in 1916 at the height of the Easter Rising. A group of angry youths on leave from the Front had smashed the windows and dropped burning rags through them, starting a fire that would have destroyed the building had the sacristan not been present to summon help.

Thank God for gentler times. Gabriel still had some fairly vociferous opponents, but these days they tended to limit themselves to turning their backs on him in the street or sending him poison-pen letters about why he and the Scarlet Whore of Babylon were doomed. Even when the subject matter was intended to hurt, the writers were so English and provincial that the letters would still be written in neat italic hand on fine paper, every word of disgust correctly spelt and grammatically appropriate to the sentence. Some even signed themselves off with "yours sincerely" or even "with kind regards and every good wish", the polite reflex enduring through the waves of sectarian loathing.

The brisk stroll to the town hall lasted nearly fifteen minutes and took Gabriel much of the way down the long street that cut the town in half. He passed the graveyard with its low stone wall, the line of metal stubs serving as a reminder of the vast metal railings that had been taken away and melted down to build Spitfires years before. Someone had put up a wooden sign to replace the metal one that had also been taken away, with the promising message etched inexpertly: *Mors Ianua Vitae*.

Gabriel noticed that some well-wisher had left fresh flowers at one of the graves and felt his belief in humanity being restored. The grave belonged to an elderly spinster who had died some years ago. According to old Fr Foley, she had died entirely alone, and only one parish stalwart attended the funeral. Someone, out of the goodness of his heart—perhaps because the old lady's anniversary was approaching

—had chosen to ensure that her grave was not neglected. Gabriel rather hoped that someone would do that little courtesy for him one day, not forgetting to say a little prayer for his suffering soul.

There was a visible social divide between one side of the street and the other. The houses on the left were large, impressive redbrick affairs, all of them with well-kept little gardens to set them back a bit from the road. The dwellings on the side of the road along which Gabriel was walking were smaller terraced cottages built for labourers and artisans. They had no gardens to separate them from passersby like his nosy self, but every pair of windows was daintily concealed by net curtains, and most had window boxes or hanging baskets that would erupt in a riot of colour in the spring.

He crossed a side street that led in the direction of the sprawling army barracks with its rows and rows of Nissen huts and perimeter fences decorated in barbed wire. If an intrepid traveller followed the path several miles farther uphill towards the plain, he would stumble upon the deserted village requisitioned by the Ministry of Defence during the war for use by the army. Some of the villagers attended his parish, having settled reluctantly nearby. They still talked bitterly about the day in 1943 when official-looking gentlemen had convened a meeting in the village schoolroom, giving the inhabitants forty-seven days to clear out. The village was in a position of strategic interest. They were promised homes elsewhere and told that as soon as the war was over they could return and rebuild their community. Gabriel had a feeling that the disgruntled former inhabitants of the village would never be allowed to resettle there; or by the time

7

they were, those houses and shops, the school building and the church would have suffered so dearly from long abandonment and the rigours of many mock street battles as to be uninhabitable.

Gabriel walked down High Street, where the little shops on both sides of the road had their blinds and shutters down and their signs and outside furnishings safely locked away inside. Trade was thriving, surprisingly in these days of "make do and mend." The town boasted a butcher, two bakeries, a greengrocer, a haberdasher and a corner shop that was not in fact on a corner but that sold everything from comic books to tins of corned beef. There were also a bookshop, more public houses than it was decent to mention and reportedly the finest tea rooms in the county.

Gabriel had a suspicion he was a little late, as there were very few people about as he crossed the road at the central crossroads and made his way up the steps through the grand blue double doors of the town hall. He was right. As soon as he stepped into the anteroom, Gabriel was accosted by Douglas Jennings, who stood awkwardly with his finger held theatrically to his lips to indicate to Gabriel not to speak above a whisper; the doors to the main hall were open, and the talk had already begun.

Douglas was a solicitor in training and looked every bit the part, from the gawkily parted hair held stiffly in place with Brylcreem to the smart if slightly archaic three-piece suit that had evidently been his father's. It had no doubt been brought out of storage when required, since clothing coupons were still in short supply, and it would be a long time before he could acquire himself a new one. Gabriel could almost smell the mothballs.

"Good evening, Father," whispered Douglas, indicating the open doors in case Gabriel had failed to work out which way he needed to go. "Pamela asked me to greet any stragglers. There are still a few seats at the back."

Gabriel nodded in acknowledgement and tiptoed into the hall, pleasantly surprised to see how full it was. There was little in the way of entertainment to be had in the small town, particularly at this time of year, nevertheless people were often reluctant to go out on cold, dark winter evenings when they could just as easily make themselves comfortable with the wireless and a good book. He recognised many faces. Some people were evidently interested in the speaker's topic, some were there to support an old friend who had returned to the town for a rare visit and some who lived alone (sadly there were plenty of those these days, many of them women) craved the presence of others and the chance of conversation after the talk, when the tea and hopefully some cake were served.

Gabriel settled himself into his seat as best he could and focused his attention on the speaker. Dr Pamela Milton, an academic in her thirties with a minor position at an Oxford college, was giving a talk about Alfred Lord Tennyson and the theme of memory. Gabriel wondered whether the subject would be a little on the lofty side for the likely audience, but he was immediately impressed by how easily Pamela seemed able to engage her listeners. It helped that she was worth looking at for any length of time. She was dressed in slacks, which Gabriel suspected did not go down well with some members of the audience, and she wore her hair short, in a style that was evidently supposed to be quite masculine but merely made her look impish, more a tomboy than a bluestocking aggressively making her way in a man's world. She wore no makeup or jewellery, but Gabriel doubted that this was carelessness on her part. Every detail of Pamela's carefully presented image was clearly intended to give the impression of a working woman—professional, no-nonsense—but in spite of her best efforts, she exuded an aura of sensuality Gabriel was not sure he was even supposed to have noticed.

"What does it mean to remember?" She almost purred, giving the audience a knowing smile that seemed to be directed personally to everyone present. "For that matter, what do we mean when we speak of keeping a person's memory alive? The very title of Tennyson's famous poem "In Memoriam" immediately provokes such a question. We make it our business to remember the dead; some of us believe we have an obligation to remember and pray for the dead. After a war in which millions have lost their lives, we are perhaps more aware than ever before of the need to remember, the need to keep alive the memories of those we have loved."

Gabriel sensed the subtle change in atmosphere, as members of the audience began to think about the people they had lost, a change Pamela had effortlessly engineered. "Arthur Hallam was Tennyson's beloved friend, tragically drowned in the prime of his life, and it was that loss Tennyson sought to understand when he set about writing his famous poem, or I should, of course, say collection of many poems. It is said to have been a favourite of Queen Victoria's, herself overcome by grief at the loss of her husband, and it is perhaps because it is part of the human condition to love, to mourn and to remember that Tennyson's words strike a chord across the decades."

The smile had been quietly replaced by a soulful expression, enhanced by the slight angle at which Pamela held her head. " 'Tis better to have loved and lost than never to have loved at all," she recited. "Consider for a moment, privately, the person or persons about whom you would write a poem if you were so inclined. Consider them whenever Arthur Hallam's name is mentioned or inferred from now on."

Gabriel felt suddenly very hot. He was not a man who blushed easily at his age, but he felt his cheeks reddening as he struggled to obey her instruction. He saw a face, faces —for who at his age and of his generation had only one loved one to remember?—but he found it impossible to allow their features to snap into focus. For the rest of the talk, Gabriel allowed himself to be distracted by Pamela Milton's expertly choreographed performance. He concentrated on the tiny details of her voice—the well-rounded vowels and the occasional creep of her West Country accent slipping back through the layers and layers of education; the strange singsong way she had of speaking that could be both commanding and flirtatious at the same time—the well-chosen yet apparently spontaneous quips and turns of phrase, her firm stride as she walked from one side of the platform to the other and occasionally left the platform altogether and stepped into the aisle that parted the audience.

'Tis better to have loved and lost . . . Gabriel was not even a fan of Tennyson, but that was one line he did know—that and *Water, water everywhere and not a drop to drink. No, that was the other chap*, he corrected himself, *the one who smoked strange things but wrote something rather lovely about Our Lady in the same poem. Keats? No, Coleridge, in "The Rime of the Ancient Mariner"*.

"We remember . . ." he heard her voice calling to him through his own confusion. "We remember because we too wish to be remembered. To keep a loved one's memory alive is as much about remembering the value of that person's life as it is a statement that we all have and deserve a place in the world, even after we have left it."

Gabriel joined in the applause, watching as George Smithson—the organiser of the event—stepped onto the platform and shook Pamela's hand enthusiastically. "Well," he said, when the applause had died down enough for him to speak. "I think we may thank Dr Milton for a most insightful talk about Tennyson. It is such a privilege to have Dr Milton with us again. As many of you know, she is a local and will be staying with her mother for some weeks over Christmas. I gather she has a book to finish." George gave Pamela an ingratiating smile. "I'm pleased to say we have a number of Dr Milton's books on sale here this evening and also in my shop—" There was a patter of laughter from the audience at the blatant advertisement. "Yes, in the bookshop, in pride of place. Dr Milton has kindly agreed to sign copies at the shop tomorrow afternoon between two and five o'clock. Now, I know it is getting late and many of you will be in a hurry to get home, but if there are any questions . . ."

There was a nervous silence as everyone in the room waited for someone else to put his hand up first. For a moment it looked as though nobody would pluck up the courage, and Gabriel was just trying to formulate a friendly question to set the ball rolling when an elderly woman stood up to speak. It was Enid Jennings, the former headmistress of the local school and personal nightmare of every inhabitant of the town under the age of forty who had not had the good fortune to be sent away for his education. She was a thin, physically unimposing woman with grey hair scraped away from a craggy face that had frozen into a permanent scowl decades ago. Her habit of constantly narrowing her eyes was quite possibly caused by failing eyesight that she refused to acknowledge, but it had the unfortunate effect of communicating contempt and displeasure before she had even opened her mouth. The change in Pamela was noticeable. She held the older woman's gaze, her jaw set as though she were clenching her teeth with the effort of having to look at Mrs Jennings at all. Her hands were clasped tightly behind her back.

"I should like to ask a question, if I may," Mrs Jennings began, in precisely the cold, faintly sneering tone one might have expected of her. "I have here a copy of an article you wrote some time ago for the journal *Mentor*, in which you dared—"

"Madam, I am not sure you are asking a suitable question for this evening," George put in quickly, sensing where things were going. "Perhaps if you were to ask Dr Milton privately—"

"Young man," Mrs Jennings interrupted, waving the offending journal in his direction, "if I wished to discuss this with Miss Milton privately, I should not have failed to do so. Since Miss Milton has been kind enough to talk for over half an hour on a subject about which none of us are interested, I'm sure it is not too much trouble for her to speak for a couple of minutes about a matter of profound importance." She glanced back at Pamela. "You wrote an intemperate article against what you term 'the antiquated teaching methods of the older generation', in which you refer to a number of such methods that feel a trifle familiar to me. Are you aware of the seriousness of defaming an individual in print?"

"You are the one making the accusation, Mrs Jennings," answered Pamela coldly, but her cheeks were flushed with either anger or embarrassment. "If you had taken the trouble to read the article, you would notice that I mention no individual by name—"

"You are not answering my question, girl," said Mrs Jennings, in the sort of tone she would have used towards an eleven-year-old miscreant she was interrogating in her study. "I said, are you aware—"

"I am perfectly aware. I stand by every word I—"

"My son is a solicitor, and he has told me—"

"Don't we all know it!" called a rasping male voice from two or three rows in front of where Gabriel was seated. "Enid Jennings, the solicitor's mother!"

George Smithson had stepped in front of Pamela like a fireman desperately trying to find a way to contain a blaze before it turns into a raging inferno. "Well, I think there are one or two other people who would like to ask Dr Milton a question about the subject of her talk. Perhaps we could—"

"I haven't finished yet!" barked Mrs Jennings, but someone at the front was standing up unbidden, revealing bodily proportions of the type that tend to bring arguments to an abrupt halt. "Excellent speech!" he called out, clapping enthusiastically. The rest of the gathering took the hint and began applauding with equal enthusiasm. Enid Jennings, who had never faced a classroom mutiny in her entire life, glanced about her in disbelief before fixing her glare on Pamela as though she, not the unnamed rugby player, had led the conspiracy against her. Pamela returned the compliment and glowered back.

"Let me get you a nice cup of tea," said George to Pamela, as the audience began to disperse and a few enthusiasts edged towards the platform to speak to her. "Don't waste your time on that old trout if she comes over; you have plenty of friends who want to talk to you."

Pamela giggled and turned to greet Dr Whitehead, a man who had known her since the stormy night long ago when he had dragged her screaming into the outside world. "Good to see that you are keeping the worthies of the town on their toes," he said with a warm smile, taking her hand unprompted to help her down from the platform. "Half the town will be wanting to read that article now, I should think. Nothing like the whiff of notoriety."

"I do hope so."

Dr Whitehead was a portly man who looked as though seniority had crept up on him all of a sudden one day, turning his hair effortlessly from brown to grey and adding a paunch to an otherwise fit, powerfully built frame. He handed Pamela a copy of one of the books George Smithson had laid out on trestle tables along the wall. "Would you do me the honour?" he asked. "I promised Therese I would bring back a copy. She was so sorry not to be able to come today, but her baby is under the weather and she didn't want to leave her mother to nurse him all evening."

Pamela took out a silver fountain pen. "I would so love to see her again, Doctor; it's been so long. I don't think I've spoken with Therese since before her pregnancy, and the baby must be—what, three or four months now?"

"Eight months. You've been away longer than you remember!" He watched Pamela as she wrote a short message for her friend on the title page and signed her name with a flourish. "I say, why don't you come to dinner one evening next week? I know you're very busy writing and all that, but the family would love to see you again and, of course, your little one."

"She's not so little either, Doctor, growing much faster than I should like. How is Therese? She wasn't too bright last time she wrote."

Dr Whitehead sighed, picking up the book and holding it open to ensure he did not smudge Pamela's writing. "A bit up and down since the birth, I'm afraid. Life's not made any easier by Freddy being away."

Pamela nodded sympathetically. "It must be very hard being an army wife. I'm not sure many people realise we're still fighting wars."

"Quite. It's hard for her not to feel a bit depressed with Christmas coming and the poor man far away."

Pamela smiled. "Don't worry, I'll cheer her up. Tell her I'm coming to make a fuss of her."

~

At the back of the hall, Gabriel considered that he really ought to buy one of the lady's books since he had come along to be entertained by her all evening. He was an avid reader of conservative tastes and had always tended to regard a book as worth reading only if its author had been dead at least fifty years, but he thought he could make an exception for Pamela Milton. He searched in his pocket for his wallet and made his way to one of the tables, picking up a copy of her latest novel, *That Singular Anomaly*, a volume the thickness and weight of a doorstop. Well, the winter evenings were so long, he thought, turning the book over for clues about its contents, but he was distracted by what sounded like a scuffle some way in front of him.

Now that she had come off the platform, Pamela's slight figure was harder to see, but as he stepped closer to her, Gabriel noticed that she was locked again in an argument with Enid Jennings, who, not satisfied with sabotaging the discussion, had come back to settle the score privately. With the background noise obscuring their conversation, Gabriel could only make out snippets of what was being said and told himself he was not really eavesdropping. They were, after all, talking in public and had to expect to be overheard at least in part.

"Worst pupil I ever had the misfortune . . . ungrateful . . . arrogant . . ."

"Late in the day . . . unqualified . . . laughable . . ."

Gabriel inched closer, nudging past the two or three people who stood between him and the conversation, before realising that he was not the only one observing the two women locking horns. They might have been a tableau of the perennial conflict between generations, particularly generations of women; the older one was bitter, tired, suppressing a lifetime of frustration, anger and envy. She was a woman in a persistent state of attrition against the world. The other was energetic, arrogant, self-assured, still acquainted with enough enthusiasm and confidence to believe that she could carve out a place for herself in the world. The women, thought Gabriel, had quite a bit in common with one another. Both were strong-minded, intelligent, independent and tenacious, but the division of not just years, but years of cataclysmic change had caused the two to be pitted against one another as no two generations had ever been before. Or perhaps it just seemed that way. Perhaps every generation believed the older or the younger did not understand their own struggles and had nothing to say to them.

"I am giving you a friendly warning, my girl," said Enid Jennings, looking every bit like Lady Catherine de Bourgh without the class or gravitas. "I destroyed your silly little life once, and I can do it again. Think very carefully before you defame me."

Pamela returned her contemptuous glance with an even stronger one of her own. "Don't threaten me, you old witch. I know exactly the sort of person you are. You have a lot more of a reputation to lose than I have."

Enid Jennings lost her temper, a few seconds, thought Gabriel, before Pamela would have done, her face flushing with rage. "Stop it!" she shrieked, far too high pitched to command any respect. "You're irrational, you always have been!" She turned her back and began walking away to make absolutely sure that Pamela could not respond, saying over her shoulder as she went, "You have been most offensive, Pamela. I really am *most* offended."

George Smithson was at Pamela's side with the tea, a rather pathetic token of appreciation under the circumstances. "Do you need a little time outside?" he asked, gesturing towards the door. "Why not have a breath of fresh air and then we can start tidying up the books?"

Pamela nodded. "Thank you, George. I'm sorry. I do

hope it hasn't spoiled the evening. I'll go outside and have a cigarette. I won't be a moment."

Gabriel glanced at George as Pamela walked away, noting that Pamela's was not the only angry face in the room. "Would you like me to check she's all right?" asked Gabriel, trying not to flinch as George began loading books into boxes with rather more violence than was necessary.

"Please do, Father," he said, in the tone of a man trying desperately to keep his cool. "I shouldn't say this, but I don't like old ladies very much. If a young man had behaved like that, he would have got a black eye from me."

"You have my sympathies. Not that I suppose I should say that."

Gabriel knew Enid Jennings, though she had not once entered his church during the months he had worked there. He knew her by reputation as a cantankerous busybody, but not in the conventional small-town sense of being the local gossip, always whispering in corners, always stirring up arguments in her desire to make the world a better place by interfering in it at every possible opportunity. No, Enid Jennings had her own brand of destructive behaviour, which made her the bane of any organising committee. Her appearance inevitably signalled the end of a happy occasion as she would go out of her way to start an argument with somebody, take issue with something or explain very loudly how very much better she could have done things, but no one cared about her enough to ask. He was almost relieved that Enid had made such a swift exit when faced with a level of opposition she had not anticipated, as it saved Gabriel from the unpleasant obligation to remonstrate with her, even though he knew it would never make any difference. Instead, he followed Pamela out to see if she required assistance.

By the time Gabriel had left the hall and the anteroom for the stone steps outside, Pamela was inhaling very elegantly from a cigarette neatly wedged into a tortoiseshell holder. She glanced up at him with a somewhat rueful look. "I hope you haven't come to give me a telling off, Father," she said, leaning back against the brick wall of the building. "She could have had the decency to stay away, couldn't she? *Vile* woman."

"I'm not sure it was wise to be quite so rude to her," suggested Gabriel, feeling as though he were walking on tiptoe across a minefield. "She's a good deal older than you."

"What the devil has that to do with it?" demanded Pamela, looking askance at him. "Where does the social convention come from that says an old person does not have to be as polite and considerate to others as everybody else? She was rude to me, she did everything possible to ruin the evening, and you suggest to *me* that I should not have been rude?"

"I said I was not sure it was wise," corrected Gabriel. "I gather she is not a pleasant woman to cross, not that I have never had the pleasure myself."

"If I were you, Father," answered Pamela, "I would stay well away from her. She brings nothing but misery and discord wherever she goes. Just because she terrorised the children of the town for years in what she laughably called a school, she imagines the world and his wife owe her a living. Please shoot me if I ever get like that."

"I most certainly will not," replied Gabriel, returning her exasperated smile with one of his own. "Much has changed in the world, but fortunately murder is still universally frowned upon." He paused, allowing her time to take another drag on her cigarette before continuing. "Would it be impertinent of me to ask what she meant when she talked about destroying your little life?"

Pamela winced violently, and Gabriel knew he had made a mistake before she responded. "I'm sorry, Father, but you had absolutely no business eavesdropping. You've got quite a nerve asking me to explain something you were never intended to hear."

"Forgive me, I'm just a little concerned for you. She appeared to be threatening you, and if she's making trouble, I was simply going to suggest—"

"Father, I am quite capable of looking after myself," interrupted Pamela sharply. "I always have done and I always will. I don't need men of any shape or form to protect me. Thanks all the same." She stubbed out the cigarette with a deft movement and returned inside to help put the hall to rights.

Gabriel watched her firm, determined tread as she moved away from him, and not for the first time in his life, he wished he had kept his mouth shut.

2

Gabriel arrived back at the presbytery to find Fr Foley dozing in his armchair by the embers of a dying fire. The old man's collapse with a heart attack had been the main reason Gabriel had been sent away from St Mary's Abbey to assist in the running of this parish, and it pleased him to see that Fr Foley had started to show signs of recovery. That said, the healing process after such a shock was lengthy, and the old man still struggled with tiredness. He seldom ventured out of an evening if he could avoid it, and in spite of the hour-long nap he took every afternoon immediately after lunch, he invariably fell fast asleep by eight o'clock or felt too dozy to be of any earthly use to anyone.

As soon as Gabriel had changed out of his wet shoes into comfortable slippers, he turned off the wireless Fr Foley had left on and stoked the fire to get it going again so that he would have some warmth as he ate his supper. When a few pathetic flames had been coaxed into life, he pottered into the kitchen, where half a pork pie had been left for him on a plate, accompanied by two pickled gherkins, some slices of tired-looking bread and a glass of cider that made up for everything else. Cider always reminded Gabriel of the abbey and the community he had not seen for so many weeks. He should not complain about the pork pie really, he told himself by way of distraction, even if he had to share the thing with another person. There had been a time when he had almost forgotten what it was like to see quite that much meat on one plate, however processed and adulterated it was, and he took it through to the sitting room so that he could eat more comfortably.

Fr Foley stirred at the sound of movement in the room, opened his eyes and looked bewilderedly at his friend. "Your spectacles are on the table beside you," said Gabriel gently, "before you mistake me for a burglar."

Fr Foley chuckled, reaching out to pick up his glasses and put them on. "You'd be the town's cheekiest burglar if you broke in, helped yourself to a meal and sat by the fire to eat it," he commented, attempting to sit a little more upright. "Did you have a pleasant evening?"

"Very interesting talk," Gabriel responded. "I suppose you know Pamela Milton?"

"Rather!" he said. "Ever such a naughty little thing, as I recall. Always in trouble with someone or other, very rarely with me, though. I'm sure she was most entertaining."

"There was quite a rumpus actually. Mrs Jennings turned up and started a row. I'm afraid it all became pretty unpleasant. Pamela was furious."

Fr Foley sighed. "Dear, oh dear, that woman is quite a menace. I've known plenty of those types over the years, tut-tutting about the length of a young girl's skirt or the shade of her lipstick and not noticing that they're consumed by pride themselves. Did you buy a book?"

"Yes, I'm sorry, but I rather felt I ought. It cannot be a very easy life, supporting oneself as a writer, and I don't suppose she earns a great deal at the university. It looks as though it might be a rather good read. She was certainly interesting enough to listen to."

Fr Foley peered at the cover. "*That Singular Anomaly.* Now where have I heard that before?"

"Gilbert and Sullivan, Father; it's from *The Mikado.* I suppose it's intended as a self-deprecating joke: that singular anomaly, the lady novelist."

"Well, she's certainly that, and not just because she scribbles for a living." Fr Foley's eyes closed with the effort of making cheerful conversation. "It's no use. I had better get to bed before I fall asleep again. Can't have you carrying me up the stairs, can we now?"

Gabriel set down his food and helped Fr Foley out of his chair, watching anxiously as he trotted through the room and up the stairs. He could not pretend he did not miss the abbey terribly on an evening such as this, and he was grateful to have at least some company to come home to when he was so unused to being alone. He reached over and switched on the wireless again to avoid sitting in silence and listened to the BBC Home Service as he finished his food. After he had locked up and taken a quick look at the following day's schedule, he thought it prudent to retire early and went to bed.

~

Gabriel was to pass a troubled night. The heavy rains that had so recently brought floods to a town inconveniently situated in a valley returned to haunt his hours of rest. It struck him as he lay in bed, listening to the hammering of raindrops against the skylight over the landing, that the rain was not quite as heavy as it sounded, magnified like that against the glass, but the recent memory of that terrible week disconcerted him. Farmland had been covered in three feet of water, autumn crops had been ruined and a young man had purportedly drowned trying to cut across the quagmire in the dark after a drunken night out with friends. All in all, it has been a ghastly time for a population that had already suffered a great deal over the past years. Being a garrison town, the area had been host to many regiments during the war years. They were stationed there just long enough for the soldiers to fall in love with the local girls before being posted to far-flung parts of the world, never to return.

Gabriel gave up trying to sleep and sat up sulkily, resenting his mind for refusing to switch off when he was in desperate need of rest. He pulled on his dressing gown and slippers and crept softly downstairs to avoid waking Fr Foley, whose room was just across the narrow landing. Long before he entered the abbey, Gabriel had established a rule that if he could not sleep for more than twenty minutes, he would get up and do something useful to make himself relax—have a hot drink or finish the crossword, some small task that would allow his mind to unwind. He had suffered insomnia much more rarely at the abbey, but then life was so much more regimented there, so much more *predictable*. He missed the very discipline of monastic life that he had struggled to obey before Abbot Ambrose had packed him off here, partly because Fr Foley needed some help and partly perhaps for his own sake, to test whether he was suited to the monastic life at all.

As Gabriel sat in the kitchen, sipping his cocoa, he thought about Enid Jennings and the scene she had caused. It rankled him that he had been relieved by her sudden exit because it had prevented him from doing the decent thing and suggesting she apologise, but the whole conversation troubled him all the more because Pamela had quite reasonably refused to discuss it with him. There had been absolutely no reason why she should have taken him into her confidence. He had demanded an explanation about words he should never have heard. Yet he had heard them, and the more he thought over that confrontation, the more his misgivings grew. He knew that people made veiled threats to one another all the time, and, as usual, he was probably making a fuss about nothing, allowing an unexpected outburst to keep him from sleep. Nevertheless, the nagging sense that something was wrong or about to become very wrong persisted.

He would visit Mrs Jennings in the morning, Gabriel told himself as he washed up the cup and saucer. For his own peace of mind, that was all. He convinced himself, as he went back upstairs to bed, that when approached on her own, Mrs Jennings might be quite amenable. Like Pamela, he suspected, she might be the sort of person who puts on a mask in public to hide a gentler, more vulnerable side. He had to battle quite hard as he dozed off to reassure himself that this was the case. After all, it was quite possible that Enid Jennings was simply a deeply nasty individual bent on upsetting everybody, who would sooner hurl a scathing reprimand at him than listen to a word he said when he appeared at her door in the morning.

It would help, thought Gabriel, if he had some harmless pretext to see her, if perhaps she had left her spectacles or her purse behind, but she had clearly left with everything that belonged to her—she was not the sort of person who could be accused of being scatterbrained. Of course, he wasn't to *know* that. In fact, he might have picked up some item or other that someone else had dropped. He might quite innocently think it were hers and be trying to be a helpful citizen by dropping round and giving it back. Fr Foley never needed his reading glasses after Mass; he always left them in the sacristy before he took his short, gentle stroll to the shops. It would hardly be stealing if he took them back again as soon as he could.

~

The whole idea felt a little more shabby next morning when Fr Foley greeted Gabriel cheerfully as they passed one another in the doorway of the sacristy and Gabriel found the reading glasses sitting obediently in their usual place on the windowsill. He took a deep breath, cursed his moral cowardice for needing such a ludicrous ruse to avoid confronting an old lady and put the glasses in his pocket.

Gabriel knew he would have to get a move on, as Mrs Jennings lived on the outskirts of the town in an isolated area that even the postman did not like visiting. He cut through a narrow footpath that took him away from the main road, past a neat little warren of cottages that ran for some half a mile before he finally emerged at the top of a wooded hill.

If it were not for the harsh chill in the air that threatened snow, Gabriel would have enjoyed the walk down a tree-lined road that slithered steeply round to a vast swathe of common land. The field resembled a welcoming green island surrounded on three sides by sparse clumps of trees that might have been thick woodland once. On the other side of the green island, where perhaps there had once also been trees, was the cottage Enid Jennings shared with her two adult children. For a moment, it was impossible for Gabriel to imagine that he might not be welcome there: the cottage looked like a picture postcard of England, exactly the sort of sweet rural abode in which a country schoolmistress ought to live, down to the thatched roof, the ivy creeping across the walls and at the far side of the building a chicken coop where four plump hens promised a rich supply of eggs for tea.

Gabriel hesitated, pondering the best way to cross the grass, which was drenched and muddy after the night's rain; then, to his right, he noticed a narrow stone path, partly shielded by trees. He began to walk more briskly, realising that he would soon be visible from the house if he were not so already, as the cover of the trees was very sparse. About two-thirds of the way along, Gabriel passed a dead tree to his left, an incongruous sight, not just because it was virtually hollow but because it stuck out some way from the other trees, encroaching a little on that flat, open green space. Gabriel guessed that it must have been left alone years ago when the land was cleared, perhaps because it had been a fine oak tree that had towered above the others, and it would have been such a pity to cut it down. It would not be missed now, of course, dead, gnarled and twisted, incapable of producing leaves in the most abundant of springs.

Gabriel could see lights on through the windows since it was such a dark morning and braced himself as he approached the door and knocked. Mrs Jennings threw open the door almost immediately, having evidently had a few minutes' warning of his approach. She gave him a look of intense suspicion. "Good morning," she said curtly, as though she could not care less what kind of a morning he was having. "How may I help you?"

On closer inspection, Gabriel noted that Enid Jennings was quite a handsome woman with strong features that must have been striking once. Her hair was very carefully combed and pinned away from her face, and she wore a choker that looked as though it may have been a wedding present or some expression of love by a long dead husband. The look of bitter disapproval, however, was as much in evidence as it had been the previous evening.

Gabriel faltered. "Good morning, Mrs Jennings," he began, resisting the temptation to clear his throat. "I saw you at the lecture yesterday evening—"

"You could scarcely have avoided that, young man," she retorted. "I intended to be noticed."

Gabriel waited to be let in, but Mrs Jennings stood planted in the doorway, giving him every possible signal that she wanted him to go away without specifically instructing him to get lost. "Well, yes—well, as it happens, someone left a pair of spectacles behind, and I rather wondered if they were yours. I was passing this way and thought I would drop them round."

Enid Jennings' mouth curled down at the corners like a lettuce starting to wither at the back of the larder. "Passing this way, were you? On your way to catechise the frogs, were you, Father? There is absolutely no place beyond this cottage you could be travelling to. There is nothing but marshland for well over a mile before you reach the Wylderlie River, and you do not appear to have a canoe about your person."

"As a matter of fact—"

"Father, there were dozens of people in that hall last night," she continued relentlessly. "Those spectacles could belong to any number of them. If that wretched girl sent you to give me a reprimand, I would warn you to mind your own business."

Gabriel threw his cards on the table. "As a matter of fact, Mrs Jennings, Pamela Milton does not know that I have come to visit you this morning. I was appalled by the scene you made yesterday; it did not seem fair to attack a guest of this town so publicly on a matter that really was no one else's concern. If you had a quarrel with her, surely it would have been better—"

Enid Jennings gave him the sort of smile that would have sent a schoolchild running for cover. "I'm sorry, Father, but you do not appear to have understood me clearly when I said that this is none of your business. Pamela Milton began this quarrel, not I. She was perfectly happy to attack me publicly in that wretched rag of a journal, and I will never forgive her for that."

"Mrs Jennings, it is very dangerous to—"

"Tell the little minx—I know perfectly well she sent you —tell the little minx that I may not write for publication, but I know how to write a letter, and I know to whom to write, so she had better enjoy her good fortune while she has it."

With that, she closed the door in his face, loudly enough to make her contempt for him as clear as possible without going so far as to slam the door shut. Gabriel had had a few doors slammed in his face and tried to be as stoical as possible as he turned his back, metaphorically shook the dust from his feet and began to walk back along the path. He had just passed the dead tree when he heard footsteps hurrying behind him and turned around to see Douglas Jennings attempting to catch up with him. Douglas had obviously been in the process of getting ready to go out to work when he had overheard the argument and dashed towards Gabriel, doing up the flapping front of his coat as he moved along.

"Father! Wait a moment!" he called, but he scarcely needed to. Gabriel stopped in his tracks and waited for the young man to catch up. "Sent you off with a flea in your ear, did she?"

Gabriel felt suddenly embarrassed and shrugged his shoulders as though he had barely noticed. "It's quite all right; it was wrong of me to intrude. I was just a little concerned about the altercation last night. It seemed wrong to walk away without attempting to patch things up. I think I'd better leave the diplomacy to someone else."

"Don't worry too much about it, Father," said Douglas, falling into step beside him. "I'm afraid those two ladies have never got on and never will. My mother expelled Pamela from her school years ago, and neither has ever forgotten it."

"Oh? Whatever for?" Gabriel could easily imagine a girl with Pamela's temperament rubbing a schoolmistress the wrong way once too often, but getting expelled from school took some effort even with Enid Jennings in charge.

"Haven't a clue, I'm afraid. Look here, I'm frightfully sorry Mother was so rude to you. It's nothing personal; she's like that with everyone. And I'm very sorry that she made such a spectacle of herself yesterday. I was going to go and see Pamela after I'd finished at the office today to apologise myself."

"Awfully decent of you. You have known Pamela a long time?"

"Almost all my life. Well, everyone knows everyone hereabouts." Douglas paused for a moment and looked over his shoulder out of what appeared to be a nervous habit. "She's older than me, of course, and boys don't really play with girls, and certainly not older girls, but she was always a character. I suppose she's what you might call a difficult customer, but she was very kind to my sister in a maternal sort of way, and we always try to meet when Pamela visits. Secretly, of course."

They were climbing the hill, which seemed very much steeper on the way up, and Gabriel found himself struggling to keep up with the younger, taller man, who was taking the incline with vast strides. "It seems a pity that a feud should have lasted so long," he commented. "They ought to be able to look back on it and laugh by now."

Douglas sighed. "My mother is very little inclined to look back and laugh at anything, unfortunately. She has rather a tendency to bear a grudge. The sad thing is, whatever it was that Pamela was expelled for all those years ago, it may not have even been important. She's quite a good girl really, always was, as I recall, but wilful women do tend to clash, and my mother certainly met her match with Pamela Milton. I have always thought, if she were a man, she would have made a very fine barrister." Douglas looked sidelong at Gabriel, mistaking his breathlessness for despondency. "Don't give it another thought, Father. I'll patch things up with Pammy.

33

Mother's going off this morning to visit her sister and won't be back until later tomorrow. I might try to persuade Pamela to come over for dinner. Agnes was hoping to see her if Mother went away."

"Does your mother go away often?"

"Oh yes, thank goodness. Her sister has a rather nice little place in Tytheminster. She's a war widow like my mother, but she has no children, so she's always been rather lonely."

"It's good of your mother to go such a distance to visit her."

"Oh, it's not far at all, or I doubt Mother would take the trouble, frankly."

Gabriel ignored the criticism. "Please forgive my ignorance. I'm afraid I have not explored the surrounding area as much as I should have done. Life has been rather busy since my arrival."

Douglas smiled. "Well, take my advice, Father. When you have a free day, treat yourself to a little trip to Tytheminster. It's only three stops on the train, and the tracks almost follow the river down to the coast. Splendid views in fine weather."

"Thank you." They had lapsed into the English habit of talking about the weather and travel to end an awkward conversation, but Douglas was clearly in a hurry to get to his office, and it was quicker at this point to turn left and cut into town farther along than to follow Gabriel back to the main road near the church. "Well, I had better let you get on. Good to talk to you."

"And you, Father. Good day."

Gabriel paused, watching as Douglas Jennings strode briskly away in the direction of petty crime, wills and boundary disputes. Feeling rather deflated in spite of Douglas' reassurance, Gabriel went about his own business, the nagging feeling of foreboding chasing him all day like a shadow at his heels.

3

Agnes Jennings stood at the kitchen window, washing up
the plates from lunch. She told herself she had no business
feeling so glum, but she had barely been able to bring herself to start clearing up in the first place, and it was only
the fear of her mother returning to a dirty house that had
prompted her to fill the sink with water and get on with
the job. She ought to be in better spirits than this; she had
enjoyed such a hearty lunch with Pamela and Douglas and
little Charlotte, who was so mature these days that it was
easy sometimes to forget that she was only a child.

Agnes would have liked to have said that it was just like
old times, except that Pamela had never come to the house
when she had lived in the town, for obvious reasons. It was
easy to forget that they had not been friends as children, as
the age gap between them was such that their childhoods
had never really overlapped. Agnes' friendship with Pamela
dated back to her own adolescence, the age at which a girl
becomes aware that she is growing up and looks to an older
female for guidance and reassurance. The world of woman-
hood could be difficult enough for any child to navigate,
but through the eyes of an immature girl fraught with in-
securities, the process of growing up had been terrifying.

Since she would never have turned to her mother for anything beyond the basic needs of life, Agnes had turned to Pamela, stifling the nagging sense that Pamela's friendship was motivated by feelings of pity for her.

It had not mattered. Pamela was different from the other girls, and best of all, Agnes' mother disapproved of her; since the enemy of one's enemy tends to become a friend, there was little to stop the friendship from growing and blossoming over the years that followed. Agnes fondly remembered counting the days to the end of term, when Pamela would arrive home from the dreaming spires of Oxford, and she could go round to Pamela's house to chat and to listen to gramophone records.

"She's a bad influence!" Agnes could still hear her mother declaring in those shrill, bitter tones—the most intoxicating words a girl could possibly hear about a friend. "You know she's a Jewess, don't you?"

"But she comes to church! We see her with her mother every Sunday."

Mother had rolled her eyes at the girl's ignorance. "What on earth has that to do with it? It's all in the blood. Grandfather, in her case. But don't tell me you haven't noticed? The features are all there, and her *colour* . . ."

Agnes slammed her fist against the draining board. This was ludicrous; she felt furious with herself for wallowing in self-pity. It was true that Douglas had disappeared off to his local with a chum immediately after they had finished eating, conveniently leaving her to deal with the tidying up, but Pamela had offered repeatedly to help, and she had refused, saying it was quite all right and she could manage. Agnes was too embarrassed to admit to Pamela that she was refusing her offer of help only because she could not risk having her friend in the house when her mother got home, which could be any time after three o'clock.

It was the shame of it, the humiliation of having to be secretive about inviting a friend to the house for lunch! The outrage of still feeling frightened enough of her own mother to go to such efforts to hide things from her! Agnes was a grown woman, a schoolmistress no less. She had an income of her own, but here she was, still living with a mother for whom she had never felt the slightest affection or loyalty. Agnes put the last of the plates on the draining board and filled the kettle with water. She glanced at the clock. It was later than she had realised—nearly four o'clock, the time at which she would normally be turning the lights on, as it grew dark so early at this time of year, but it had been such a dreary day that she had had the kitchen light on since late morning.

Not for much longer, Agnes consoled herself, drying the crockery and shoving it into the cupboard with as much haste as she could risk without breaking anything. Everything was about to change; she simply had to pluck up the courage. Precisely how frightening could an old lady be, even her mother? What was the worst she could do to her now that she was an adult and had a modicum of protection from the law? Agnes looked across the grass and felt her heart sink at the sight of her mother walking slowly but determinedly down the path, disappearing from time to time behind a tree. Agnes watched with the steadiness of a sniper peering at a hostile figure through his gun sights. Then the sound of the kettle whistling made her jump, and she moved quickly to the stove to switch off the gas and fill the teapot.

When she returned to the window, she could not see her mother at all; then she felt her heart starting to race. The path was empty. There was no sign of anyone walking along it or even any sign that anyone had ever walked that way. Agnes clasped the edge of the sink to steady herself, letting out a breathless whimper nobody heard.

~

An hour later, Douglas returned to the house, pleasantly filled with beer and warmed by a happy afternoon of good company. He should not have delayed his return home until after dark; it always made the last part of his journey so much more irksome. But it had been such gloomy weather anyway that he had found himself lingering near the roaring fire at The Old Bell, keeping his back to the ever-darkening street on the other side of the steamed-up windows.

It really was time and gone time for him to get a place of his own. Douglas told himself as much every single time he reached the point in his journey home where the pavements and the habitations of the town gave way to raw, uncultivated countryside that only William Wordsworth could have appreciated. It was not his first plan to hang around in this little town once he was fully qualified; Bath or Salisbury would be the obvious places to go, but even if he stayed, he ought at least to look for a bachelor pad a little closer to civilisation. One of those houses on the terrace near the school would suit him perfectly.

Douglas' good spirits disintegrated almost immediately as he came into view of the house in the distance and were replaced by a cold, creeping sense of dread. He always carried a torch with him when he knew he might be back after dark, as there was no lighting around the house on account of its isolated location, but he did not need to be able to see much to know instinctively that something was amiss. Looking through the pitch darkness across the grass, he could see the distant light from the kitchen window, which should have been welcoming, but he sensed that the house was empty, and it should not have been at that time of day. It was partly the fact that there was no light coming from any other window but mostly just the raw gut feeling of a trained soldier that all was not as it should be.

Douglas swallowed a wave of anxiety, shone his torch along the path and began to walk towards the house. He had never been of a nervous disposition as a boy, but there was nothing like a brief, disastrous military career and a troubled conscience to leave a man with an exaggerated sense of danger; he felt childishly unsettled by the shadows created by the powerful beam of light and the usually familiar noises of a December night. There was a creaking of bare branches all around, the sound of his own footsteps crunching twigs and grit as he walked; there was a whispering of the wind, always magnified in this spot because of the tunnel effect created by the lie of the land. He knew he was being foolish. The kitchen light was the only one switched on because Agnes had not yet left the kitchen, poor girl. Nothing more. Nothing worse than that.

Then Douglas heard a moaning noise; a soft, eerie wail clearly not produced by an animal, which began very softly only to crescendo as he drew nearer the source. He looked about him for some means to protect himself, reached out wildly and snapped a branch from a nearby tree. His army training told him it was not much of a weapon, but it was as long as a walking cane and thick enough not to break easily if he had to use it to fight off an attacker. Douglas stepped cautiously towards the sound, feeling the soft grass under his shoes as he left the path.

He had scarcely gone ten paces when a hand grabbed his ankle, throwing him into a state of panic. Douglas wrenched himself free and gave his assailant a sharp kick; he felt the toe of his shoe strike the soft tissue of a human face before he staggered back, resisting the urge to make a run for it. "Who's there?" he shouted, shining the torch in the direction of the now hunched figure before him. He could feel tiny splinters prickling the palm of his hand as he clenched his weapon. "Get up!"

That was when he saw her. Curled up in the foetal position, shivering and struggling for breath, lay Agnes. Douglas dropped to his knees immediately, pulling her hands away from her face. He could feel the sticky wetness on her fingers and knew from the bitter, metallic smell that it was blood. "Help me!" she sobbed. "Oh please, I'm so cold!"

Douglas battled to pull Agnes to her feet, holding her by the wrists to avoid having to touch the blood again; his stomach was in knots as it was. "My God, Agnes, what have you done?"

～

It had undoubtedly been a mistake to call the police, thought Douglas, but under the circumstances he had not been able to think of a more appropriate course of action. He had relaxed a little once Agnes had washed her hands and collected herself sufficiently to accept a glass of brandy. It turned out that the blood on Agnes' hands was, in fact, hers, emanating from her nose, thanks to the kick from Douglas as he had attempted to escape his invisible aggressor. Douglas suspected almost immediately that the two of them had—separately, it appeared—been victims of their own imaginations. He had convinced himself that there was danger in the woods because Agnes had wandered out of the house and made it look deserted; it was dark and cold, and he was probably rather drunk. Even his momentary belief that Agnes had killed someone looked absurd when he gave it a moment's thought. On Agnes' part, she had convinced herself that she had seen her mother walking along the path and then apparently vanishing into thin air. Since their mother had not returned home as planned and it was most unlike her to be late, however, Douglas had taken the precaution of informing the police.

The constable who came belligerently to the door took a statement from Agnes and a rather shorter statement from Douglas before letting forth a sigh as though to leave neither of them in any doubt that he would rather be doing anything else on a Saturday evening than talking to them. The situation was rendered worse by the fact that Agnes had a dreamy way of talking when she was distressed that made it seem as though she were slipping in and out of a trance, which hardly helped the case for her sanity.

"Let me see if I've got this straight," said the constable, poring over the notes he had made in his book. "Miss Jennings was not the victim of an assault because the bloody nose she received from you, Mr Jennings, was the result of an accidental blow to her face dealt because you believed her to be in the process of attacking you."

"It wasn't a blow, it was a kick," Douglas interrupted, "and it wasn't even a deliberate kick, come to that. I was trying to shake her off and my shoe collided with her face."

"Indeed," answered the constable dryly. "Could happen to anyone. Now, Miss Jennings, you say that you were looking out of the kitchen window not long after four o'clock when you saw your mother walking up the path. You were distracted for a moment by the kettle whistling, and when you returned to the window she had disappeared. She never came to the house."

"I know how mad it sounds," said Agnes, who honestly could not have looked madder under the circumstances if she had tried. Her face was pale and pinched with anxiety, her eyes were red from weeping and her clothes were damp and dirty from her lying outside on the ground. Douglas wished he had urged her a little more strongly to get changed before the police arrived, but even if she had bathed, dressed in her finest and kept her composure throughout the entire interview, her nose—bruised and swollen, still bearing traces of dried blood—made her look like a crazed Dickensian match girl. Her appearance might elicit sympathy, but she hardly had the makings of a credible witness.

"Might I ask what you were doing on the ground in the first place?" enquired the policeman. "Did you lose your footing in the darkness perhaps?"

Agnes did not appear to notice that he was suggesting an innocuous explanation to her. "I'm afraid I'm not sure how I got down there. I think I must have blacked-out or something. I'm afraid I do that sometimes."

"Really?"

"Look here, constable," Douglas broke in, "my sister is not in the best of health. She is rather prone to fainting and dizzy spells."

"Indeed?" He looked back at Agnes. "Might you perhaps have taken a funny turn at the window then?"

"Yes," said Douglas before Agnes could find her voice. "That might well have happened, now that I think about it. What do you say, Aggie?"

Agnes ignored her brother's steely glance in her direction. "I'm sure that didn't happen."

"But how could you be sure?" The constable noticed Agnes opening her mouth to challenge him and continued. "We may have to assume that you were mistaken when you looked out of the window, Miss Jennings. It was getting dark, you were expecting her back at about that time so you imagined that you saw her. An easy enough mistake to make."

"How is it an easy mistake to make?" Agnes demanded, suddenly coming to life. "How likely is it that I accidentally saw my mother walking towards me? I'm certain I saw her." She looked at Douglas for support, but he stared fixedly at the hearth rug. "Well, surely you believe me? Why would I make up a story like this?"

Douglas turned to the constable, whom he had met on a number of occasions going about his lawful business; he decided it was time to steer the conversation in a more reasonable direction. "PC Davenport, I realise this all sounds

45

rather incredible to you, but one thing we are certain about is that our mother is missing. We expected her back hours ago—even four o'clock was a little late for her—but we are very concerned that she has not returned by now. Whatever has happened, she is not where she ought to be."

Davenport relaxed almost imperceptibly. "Isn't it possible that she might have decided to stay at her sister's another night perhaps? They may have been enjoying a jolly day out and lost track of the time. Before they knew it, she had missed the last train and decided to wait until the morning to return home. She's a grown woman; she's at liberty to make a last-minute change of plan."

"It would be very out of character for our mother to do that," Douglas stressed. "She was not really the sort of person who made last-minute changes of plan." He could not honestly imagine his mother having a jolly day out either, for that matter, but that was hardly worth sharing.

"Have you telephoned your aunt to ask if she is still there?"

Douglas raised his eyes to heaven. "She has no telephone, or of course we would have checked before troubling you. Look, if she did arrive back in the town, people will have seen her. The stationmaster could tell you whether she got off the train at this station. It can hardly be beyond the wit of man to go to my aunt's house and check in person if she is still there?"

"Well—"

"If the police are too busy with the small matter of my mother's disappearance, I can go and check tomorrow."

"Yes, thank you, Mr Jennings," Davenport responded,

getting up to leave. "There are certainly a few enquiries we can make; don't trouble yourself about that. If it's not too impertinent, I would suggest it might have been better to call a doctor than a policeman."

Douglas propelled Davenport in the direction of the sitting-room door. "Get out!" he snapped. "There is absolutely nothing wrong with my sister's mind. If she says she saw our mother walking towards the house, she saw her. Now you had better make sense of this little puzzle, constable. A woman is missing, and her life may well be in danger."

When Douglas had seen PC Davenport out, he locked the door with a little more care than usual, making sure the key clicked twice as it turned in the lock, then pushing across the two stiff, heavy bolts as an added precaution. It was pointless, he thought, as he gave the door a last rattle. A burglar could quite easily smash a window, and they were far too isolated for anyone else to notice, but he felt the need to fortify his castle. He could hear Agnes sobbing in the sitting room and groaned. Since the war, Douglas had felt a constant sense of his own helplessness, and he did not believe that he would ever shake it off. He stepped closer to the sitting room, watching as Agnes curled up on the sofa, her face buried in her lap, her arms wrapped around her knees. He was overwhelmed by a wave of nausea. "Aggie, stop it!" he hissed, but she did not acknowledge him. "Please don't, nobody's hurting you. You—you can't stand her! Nobody can!"

When Agnes continued to ignore him, lost in her own grief or confusion, Douglas turned on his heel, slammed the sitting-room door shut and stormed upstairs to his room.

47

I'm turning into my mother, he thought bitterly, throwing himself onto his bed. *Hiding fear behind rage like the louse I am.* It was so much easier to be angry.

4

Monday morning dawned crisp and cool but without bringing the heavy snow for which the children had been desperately waiting. Gabriel stopped at the bookshop on his way
to buy the morning paper, keen to discover whether George
Smithson had received the copy of Newman's *Apologia* he
had ordered weeks ago. The bookshop was a favourite haunt
of Gabriel's; it reminded him in some ways of the monastic
library, with its seemingly endless bookshelves heaving with
knowledge and plenty of little cubbyholes in which to sit
and leaf through a volume or two before buying anything.
It was not as peaceful and quiet as a library, with the bell
over the front door jangling every time a customer came in
so that George would know to come into the shop if he
were in the back room making himself a cup of tea. George
was kept mercifully busy, but even if people talked, Gabriel
noticed that customers in bookshops tended to whisper as
they would in a library, almost as though they feared to dis-
rupt the serious atmosphere of the place.

The shop was relatively quiet on a Monday morning,
but Gabriel saw that George had company. A little girl in a
gingham dress and a thick red cardigan sat on the counter,

swinging her legs as she chatted easily with George. Gabriel guessed that she was about nine years old and noted the resemblance immediately; she looked exactly as he imagined Pamela must have looked once; long dark plaits hanging forward over her shoulders, a lovely Madonna face, so perfect it could have been painted, and a knowing smile she had also inherited from her mother. He stood on the doormat, not wishing to intrude upon the conversation, but they stopped talking immediately and glanced in his direction. Only when they were silent did Gabriel register that they had been speaking in French.

"I am most impressed," said Gabriel to the child, as he approached the counter. "Your French is excellent."

The child jumped down from the counter, turned and picked up the copy of *The Wind in the Willows* she had been leafing through—it had evidently been their chosen topic of conversation—before giving Gabriel her full attention. "Not as excellent as Mummy would like," she said with a mischievous giggle. "Mr Smithson is helping me with my accent."

Gabriel held out a hand to her. "You must be Charlotte," he said. He expected her to shake his hand, but to his surprise, she kissed it instead, an act of piety he had not quite anticipated from the daughter of the town's mischief maker. He chided himself for making an unfair judgement. "Are you here for the holidays? The schools haven't broken up for Christmas yet."

"I learn at home," explained Charlotte. "Mummy says schools are just bastions of conformity."

Gabriel struggled to suppress his laughter; there was something very endearing about listening to a child enunciating concepts she did not understand and could only just pronounce. "I see."

"I tell you what, Scottie," said George, "why don't you go into the kitchen and get yourself something to drink? Your mother left your milk in the fridge for you. You know where the glasses are."

Charlotte gave him a sidelong look that made it quite clear she knew she was being got out of the way, but she trotted out of sight happily enough as if to say, "You good people are too boring for me anyway."

"Why do you call her that?" asked Gabriel, as soon as the child was out of earshot. "No Scottish blood there, is there?"

George smiled before disappearing behind the counter. "Her nickname started out as Chottie. If you think about it, there aren't many shortenings of Charlotte, either Charlie or Lottie, and Pamela didn't really like those very much." He reemerged, heaving onto the counter a large box, which he began cutting open. "So she was Chottie until a couple of years ago, when she was given a tartan beret as a birthday present, which she refused to take off for about six months, according to Pamela. You know the way small children get attached to things sometimes? The first time I saw her dressed like that, I said, 'You're not Chottie, you're Scottie,' and somehow it just stuck. She has outgrown the beret, or it was lost or became too ragged to wear anymore, but she can't seem to lose the name. Now—" George began taking out and unwrapping his latest haul of books. "These arrived first thing this morning, thank goodness. Can't have

Mr Pitman coming in yet again wondering if his copy of Aristophanes' *The Birds* has arrived."

"Perish the thought. Any sign of my—"

"Aha! Here we are." George pulled out Newman's *Apologia* with the panache of a magician pulling a rabbit out of a hat. "Yours, I believe?"

Gabriel was busy inspecting the bindings as George opened his sales book and wrote down the details when the bell chimed with unexpected violence, causing them both to stop what they were doing and look in the direction of the noise. Douglas Jennings was standing on the doormat, the door left gaping open. "Thank God you're here, Father!" he exclaimed without further introduction. "Fr Foley said he thought you'd come this way."

"For goodness' sake, come in and close the door!" insisted George. "You'll freeze us all to death."

"Sorry," murmured Douglas, pushing the door shut in what was almost embarrassment. "I'm so sorry, Father, but I couldn't think of anyone else to ask. Mother's gone missing; she did not return home as expected after her visit to her sister's. The police are being absolutely ghastly about it, and poor Agnes is beside herself. She keeps saying she saw Mother approaching the house. The police are treating her like a lunatic, and I'm beginning to think they have a point. I know this isn't really a spiritual matter but—"

"Of course, I'll go and see her," said Gabriel simply, putting Douglas out of his misery. "Is she at home?"

"Yes, I don't really like to leave her alone for very long in the state she's in, but I had to find you. I've already been to the school to ask Mrs Howse to take Aggie's class for her, and I really should be at work myself. I'm terribly late as it is, and Mr Pitman is such a stickler for punctuality. I shall be up half the night catching up with everything I'm missing this morning."

"I suspect Mr Pitman might make an exception to the rule under the circumstances."

"I hardly think so; we have to be in court tomorrow."

Gabriel turned to George as they opened the door to leave. "I wonder if you could ask Charlotte—Scottie—to run down the road to the presbytery and tell Fr Foley I have been called out on an urgent matter? Would that be all right?"

"I don't mind at all, Father," came a bright voice from the door to the back of the shop. Charlotte had evidently overheard every single word of the conversation and wanted them to know it. "You have been called out on an urgent matter. Is that right?"

"Yes." As Gabriel and Douglas left the shop, Gabriel realised he had forgotten about his book. He opened the door again. "I'll return for the book later," he told George before following Douglas out into the street. "I hope it was all right sending that little one off on an errand. She can't be more than about nine, I suppose, but she's so articulate, one almost forgets."

"Oh, she'll be quite all right," agreed Douglas. "It will take only five minutes, and she'll enjoy the walk. But bear in mind, Scottie's only seven. She's quite tall for her age, and she's growing up surrounded by adults. That's why she seems so much older. Anyway—"

"Yes, I'm sorry. Fill me in on the details as we go."

"Well, it's better if you hear it from Agnes, of course," Douglas began, "but what I can tell you is that Mother definitely arrived in town on Saturday afternoon, as she had planned. When we first reported her missing, the constable was inclined to think she had decided to stay at her sister's a little longer and been unable to get word to us. Frankly, they were not very interested. It hardly helped that Agnes was making no earthly sense, and the constable left making half-hearted promises that he would make a few enquiries. But then, when Mother failed to return home the following day, I travelled to my aunt's house myself, and she told me categorically that my mother had left at her usual time. After some pestering, the police were prevailed upon to take the situation seriously, and they found out from the station-master that Mother had been seen getting off the train and leaving the station."

"Where were you that afternoon, if I may ask?" enquired Gabriel.

"I had an early lunch at home—Pamela and Scottie joined us, but I left shortly afterwards to have a drink at The Old Bell with a friend. A dozen people will vouch that I was in that pub, not that I suspect it will come to that. I hope I don't sound unsociable, Father, but I felt rather outnumbered at the lunch table with three females talking at me. You know the way it is."

Gabriel smiled. "I can well imagine. Was Agnes alone around the time your mother was expected back?"

"Yes." Douglas frowned over his shoulder in the direction of Gabriel's limping figure. "You know something, Father, you really ought to take more exercise! Look at you huffing and puffing, and we're going downhill. I shall have to drag you back up the hill on a hurdle at this rate."

"That really is in awfully bad taste," remarked Gabriel,

but he suspected the martyr's crown was never likely to be his. "I'm quite fit really for a man of my great age. When I was at the abbey, I walked to and from the village all the time. Getting back to the case in hand, Agnes was alone?"

"Yes, she couldn't possibly have risked Mother coming home to find Pamela in the house. She would have made very sure her guests had left in good time for her to clear up and put the house to rights before Mother's return. I rather wish she hadn't been alone now, an independent witness might have been able to make more sense of this." They were walking along the path to the house now. Douglas gestured a little to his left. "That was where I found Agnes," he explained, "or rather, she found me. I feel rather ashamed of myself; to be honest, I didn't realise it was her grabbing hold of me and gave her rather a kick. I'm amazed I didn't break her nose."

"You didn't realise who it was?"

"Father, I didn't even realise it was a woman. I'm not sure what I thought had taken hold of me. I'm ashamed to say I panicked. You honestly don't think I would have hurt her on purpose, do you?"

Gabriel could see Agnes' plaintive face staring at them from the kitchen window and quickened his pace. As they grew closer, the unfortunate incident of Saturday night became painfully obvious. Agnes' face was quite badly bruised. "I'm sure it was an accident," offered Gabriel. "Let us not get distracted from the real mystery here."

Agnes let them in wordlessly and moved automatically towards the kitchen so that she could make a pot of tea, but Douglas placed a hand gently on her arm and gestured for her to take Gabriel into the sitting room. "Don't worry about tea, Aggie," he said softly. "Why don't you tell Father what's happened and I'll make the tea."

Agnes nodded and walked through the sitting-room door without looking back to see if Gabriel had followed. Even though Agnes and Douglas were his parishioners, Gabriel had never entered this house on a friendly call. Fr Foley had warned him against doing so due to Enid Jennings' having lapsed in typically acrimonious style over a year before, thanks to some detail of parish politics too petty to be remembered now. Agnes and Gabriel entered a comfortable if claustrophobic room, the meeting place of a cottage that must have belonged to a farming family before the land had to be sold off and the cottage became merely an inconveniently placed dwelling for a family who preferred to live apart from the world. The walls were clad in wood panelling for the sake of keeping the heat in, and on them hung a number of pictures and mementos, including a mounted fox's head, which the taxidermist had fashioned with a snarl as though the unfortunate creature's final act towards his killers had been one of angry defiance.

"Please sit down, Father," said Agnes, gesturing towards a creaky old leather armchair, which Gabriel suspected was the most comfortable chair in the room. He waited a moment for her to sit down on the sofa before sitting down himself. "I'm so sorry to drag you out here. It's just that I don't really know who else to talk to, and I know the police think I'm crazy or making things up. In fact, if I didn't know better, I would say that Douglas thinks I'm a raving lunatic too, but he's too polite to say so to my face."

"Agnes, I'm sure you're not mad," said Gabriel and he meant it. He knew that Agnes was very well respected at the school in spite of her tender years and that parents spoke highly of her skills. He doubted very much that a girl barely out of school herself would run quite such an orderly and successful class if she were not in full possession of her mental faculties. That said, he had not assured her that she was not troubled because mere observation made that quite obvious. "Now, why don't you tell me exactly what happened? Don't think about what I'm likely to make of the whole thing; just tell me in your own words exactly what you saw on Saturday afternoon. I'm sure there's nothing we can't puzzle out between us."

Agnes gave a nervous smile. She was a plain, dull-looking young woman with a thin, sunken face framed by wispy, mouse-coloured hair, but there was a vulnerability about her that made it very difficult not to warm to her immediately. "I hardly know how to start," she said quickly, then closed her eyes as though she preferred to pretend he was not there. "I was just finishing the washing-up. Pamela and her little one had come for lunch, and I needed to have everything back in its proper place before Mother came home. She doesn't like Pamela—well, that's not very important at the moment. I was just finishing and had put the kettle on to make some tea when I noticed Mother in the distance."

"You were looking out of the kitchen window, I presume?" confirmed Gabriel. Agnes' rapid, breathless way of talking made her quite difficult to understand at times, a problem vastly exaggerated by her recent injury, which forced her to breathe through her mouth. "What time was it?"

Agnes was momentarily confused at being asked two questions one after the other. "Yes, I was looking out of the window, almost daydreaming really. As it happens, I looked at the clock because I suddenly noticed how dark it was outside and suspected it was later than I had thought. It was approaching four o'clock, a little later than I would have expected Mother back, but not much later. I tell you she was there; I could see her in the distance, walking along that path. You know the path I mean; you have walked that way yourself. I heard the kettle whistling and moved away to switch off the gas and make the tea. I was gone only a moment, but when I got back to the window she had disappeared.''

Gabriel leaned back in his chair. He had no doubt at all that she was sincere; she certainly believed she had seen her mother there. ''When you say you saw your mother coming up the path, can you be absolutely sure it was she? As you have said, it was already dusk, and she would have kept disappearing from view as she walked behind trees. Are you absolutely sure—''

''Father, I have watched my mother walk up that path a thousand times!'' she interrupted, with the beginnings of impatience. ''Yes, of course it was growing dark, that's what the policeman said, and she did keep going in and out of view as she walked past the trees, but she was never out of sight for more than a second. I thought I must have made some strange mistake at first, not because I really thought I could have seen her and not seen her—that doesn't make any sense—but because she never came to the house. There is nowhere else she could have gone if not to the house, and if something terrible had happened to her on that stretch of ground, surely she would have been found by now. Her body, I mean.''

"Indeed." Gabriel noticed that as soon as Agnes had referred to a body, she had become deathly pale, and he suspected it was the first time it had occurred to her that her mother might be dead. "I assume the police have searched the area?"

"Well, yes. Not very thoroughly, but there's not very much to search. The woodlands are very sparse around here; there really aren't many places she could be. I tried to search for her myself."

"Is that why Douglas found you on his way home?"

Agnes' eyes glistened and she nodded hastily, choking on the answer. She took a long breath in and out before attempting to speak further. "I didn't know what to do. I was all alone in the house. I had no idea when Douglas would be back, and it was all so . . . so *creepy*. It felt like something out of a horror story. I knew I had seen her, but nobody disappears into thin air. When she didn't come to the house, I think my imagination got the better of me; I thought that something must have happened. I guessed that she must have been taken ill and fainted. I would have seen her lying on the ground, but it was the only thing I could think of." Agnes paused to catch her breath. "Now that I think about it, she was walking quite slowly. I rushed out of the house without even putting my coat on—I suppose I thought I would be only a minute—and then went to the place I thought I had last seen her."

Gabriel looked across at Agnes, but she had screwed her eyes up tight to restrain herself—a second too late—and tears had begun coursing down her face. "Agnes, you must tell me everything. What did you see out there?"

"Nothing," she whimpered. "That was the trouble; I saw

nothing. There was no sign of her at all, not a thing. I don't know if there were even footprints. I wouldn't have been able to see them in that light, and by the morning there had been all that rain. But she would have left some sign she had been there, and there was nothing. And then the strangest thing happened to me."

Gabriel heard the creak of the floorboards, turned around and noticed that Douglas was standing in the doorway, holding a tea tray, evidently trying to avoid interrupting Agnes. Gabriel signalled to him to sit down and pulled out of his pocket a clean handkerchief, which he handed to Agnes. He had lost many handkerchiefs over the years in such situations, but since they were an enduringly popular Christmas present for a celibate male, he never ran out. "It's all right, Agnes. You are quite safe."

"I am more afraid of myself than you, Father," she sobbed. "The thing is, I must be mad. I can't explain what happened next at all. I really did feel as though I were possessed."

Gabriel could not help sitting up sharply at the word. He did not dare look at Douglas, whom he expected was clasping his head in vexation. "Possessed?"

"It is the only word I can use; it was as though some dark force were descending upon me as I stood there. I thought I was going to be sick; I started shaking and weeping. It was freezing cold, but I was perspiring as though I were in the middle of the desert. I've never felt anything like it. I really thought I was going to die. I just collapsed. I think I may have fainted, because the next thing I knew, it was completely dark and I had no idea where I was."

"And that was when Douglas came along?"

"Yes."

"Well, that would explain why you did not attempt to call out to him."

"I suppose that's one mystery solved," declared Douglas, slightly too acerbically. Agnes winced with shame. "You know, when I saw the blood on her hands, I thought for one terrible moment it was someone else's."

"For pity's sake, what sort of a person do you take me for?" cried Agnes, in a flash of temper that seemed out of character. "Did you honestly think I had killed someone?"

Douglas raised his hands defensively. "I'm—I'm sorry, I really have no idea what I was thinking. Look—" It was his turn to look ashamed. "Look here, Father, I'm sorry. I'm not sure quite what got into me. During the war, I was captured on a night raid, and I've never been too keen on walking through undergrowth in the dark ever since. There was just something very spooky about that path after dark. When Agnes grabbed me, I lost my head. That's all there is to it; I lost my head. I realised very quickly that the blood was hers."

Gabriel closed his eyes, considering what they had said. It was the sort of tantalising conundrum that would have excited him ordinarily, but he was sobered by the thought that a missing woman—however unpleasant—was at the heart of this and that whether or not Agnes and her brother had considered it, the likelihood was that Enid Jennings was dead. He remembered his old adversary Detective Inspector Applegate telling him once that, in his judgement, if a person was reported missing and there were no reasons to believe the person had disappeared of his own accord, there was a window of forty-eight hours in which the person might be found alive. After that, the police were looking for a dead body.

"Agnes," he said finally, standing up. "Why don't you show me the place yourself? It would be useful to get the lie of the land in daylight anyway."

Agnes could not hide her reluctance. "Father, the police have already been round, I told you. It didn't even take them very long; they just shuffled about for an hour or so. In fact, with a pair of binoculars, you could probably see if anything were amiss without even coming down the hill. They haven't found her; they haven't found any sign of a—a—"

"Grave?" Douglas put in.

"I was going to say 'struggle'," she responded with a faint tone of accusation.

"Sorry. Why not take a look? We can have the tea afterwards. It shan't get cold."

~

Gabriel had, of course, walked this way in daylight quite recently, but he realised just how preoccupied he had been with worrying about the reception he might receive to notice anything important. Now, he employed his keenest powers of observation, mentally noting any detail he thought might be relevant. As Agnes had pointed out, the bad weather had blotted out any sign of footprints, but he doubted there would have been very much to go on anyway. The area had been badly affected by the recent flooding, and the ground still felt tacky and unstable from having been waterlogged, like the surface of a vast, dirty sponge.

"The house was not flooded?" asked Gabriel absently. "It doesn't look as though your house suffered damage from those terrible floods."

"What has that to do with anything?" demanded Douglas, with the irritability of a man whose precious time is being wasted. "The floodwaters cleared weeks ago." He looked at Gabriel to see if he was satisfied with the answer, which he clearly was not. "Well, as a matter of fact, we got away quite lightly. There haven't been floods like that in this area since long before my mother was born. The land is low-lying, but we're quite some distance from the river. Mother always said that if floods ever did come, though, our house might suffer, so she bought a whole lot of sandbags from the barracks. After the war there wasn't very much call for them, thank goodness; they must have practically given them to her. When Mother got word that the floodwaters were coming our way, she got Agnes and me to stack dozens of the things up against the door and the windows. When the water started pouring down that hill, she even got us to barricade in the door from the inside so that there were two walls of sandbags to protect us. The area around the door needed a lick of paint afterwards, but she was right. The house didn't flood."

"She was certainly a practical woman," commented Gabriel and bit his tongue. "I mean *is*. She showed a great deal of forethought."

"We'd certainly have been flooded, but in fact the waters did not come up very high in the end. It is not easy to see from down here, but the ground undulates quite a bit. The house is some inches above where we stand now."

"This was where I saw her," said Agnes, as though trying

63

to remind the two men of why they were there. "That was where I lost sight of her."

She was standing facing the house, the dead, hollow tree directly to her left. "You're absolutely sure that was where she was standing?" asked Gabriel.

"Yes, because I could see that tree from the window. You can see that it looks different from the others."

Gabriel moved over to where she was standing and took a closer look at the tree. It was more than just hollow, it was practically a shell of a tree. But though there might be space for a person to hide himself in it, there was no obvious place for him to go from there other than back onto the path, where he would be in full view of the kitchen window. He got down on his knees and examined the ground in and around the tree and then stood up and looked at the path and the marshy grass on either side.

"What were you trying to see in there?" enquired Douglas, pointing at the hollow tree Gabriel had just left alone. "A secret trapdoor? I think you'll find none of the stones on that path will come loose either."

"That was not at all what I was looking for," Gabriel retorted. "We are very far from the realms of a children's adventure story, I'm afraid. That's a point—" He suddenly realised what was disturbing him so much. It was just too deserted there, too silent. The rest of the town was really no distance from the spot; within minutes, any fit man at a brisk walk could reach the nearest house, and yet the place felt so much more isolated than it really was, so *dead*. "This is common land, isn't it?" he asked. "Anyone can come here."

"Yes," said Agnes, "the cottage was a farmhouse once; all the surrounding land would have belonged to it, though I don't suppose it was terribly easy to farm. It's pretty gloomy down here even in warm weather. We own about half an acre, but it's all round the other side. From here to the town, I suppose it belongs to the people of the town. Why do you ask?"

"I was just wondering why one never sees any children playing here, for example. On the rare occasions I strike out into the countryside from the other side of the town, I quite often see little groups of children running around, having picnics, climbing trees. That sort of thing. Not much for them to do in town, so they run wild. But not around here."

Agnes laughed. It was the first time Gabriel had ever heard her laugh, and he felt a little sheepish at being the cause of it. "What self-respecting urchin is going to play under the watchful gaze of the town's dreaded schoolmistress?" she asked, not unreasonably. "In any case, there's an old rumour that the place is haunted."

"Nonsense, of course," Douglas cut in, in a tone that would have been pompous in an older man. "Just little-town superstition, as usual. There is an old story that a man hanged himself here many years ago. The story goes that he violated and murdered a child. The people of the town found out who he was and would have lynched him, so he hanged himself, apparently from that very tree."

"When is that supposed to have happened?"

"It never happened, Father; it's a fanciful story. There is no record of any man committing suicide in this area or of any child being abducted and killed like that. Not for the past hundred years at least. As I said, it's nonsense. My mother's presence was frightening enough for children without having to scare them away with ghost stories. Even we never played out here."

Then where did you play, Douglas? thought Gabriel, as they walked back to the house and the promise of tea and biscuits. *What sort of childhood did the two of you have in this dank, moated grange of a home?*

5

That evening, Gabriel was walking up the high street after a house call when he noticed that the lights were still
on in Douglas Jennings' office. He suspected that the poor
man was staying on late to catch up with the work he had
missed that morning and should probably not be disturbed,
but Gabriel had been puzzling over the events of the week-
end for much of the day. The urge to find out if there had
been any further developments was irresistible.

Douglas let Gabriel into the office, the secretary having
long gone home, and as they climbed the stairs Gabriel could
not help noticing the smell of alcohol and the unsteady gait
Douglas was attempting to hide. "I see you have not been
in the office all evening," Gabriel commented, when they
reached the top of the stairs. "Should you really be working
under the influence?"

"I'm not a High Court judge, Father," snapped Douglas,
with the petulance of a schoolboy caught with his hand in
the sweetie jar. He showed Gabriel into his office. "If you
must know, I popped out earlier for ten minutes to fortify
myself. I'm not in the habit of drinking on the job, and I
would appreciate it if you could keep this to yourself."

"How is Agnes?"

"The same as when you saw her last, I suppose." He sat down heavily at his desk and discreetly turned over some papers. "I left for work not long after you left. I have to get on with things somehow, but I oughtn't to leave her alone in that house really. There could be a murderer on the loose, for all we know."

"Is it your belief that your mother has been murdered?" asked Gabriel. "I take it the police have not found anything yet."

"They've not found her, if that's what you mean." Douglas gave an apologetic sigh and dropped his head into his hands. Gabriel doubted he had had a wink of sleep in two nights. "I'm sorry, Father. I'm not a criminal lawyer by training, but I do know something of the way these cases pan out. If she were alive, she would have been in touch by now. Whatever else she was, she was not unreasonable like that. If she had taken it upon herself to walk away, she would at least have let us know."

"You don't believe Agnes' story, do you? You made it rather too obvious this morning."

Douglas opened a drawer and pulled out a silver cigarette case, which he offered to Gabriel. Gabriel declined. "Well, what do you think? The ghost of a hanged child murderer snatched my mother from Agnes' sight? I'd credit you with a little more sense than that."

Gabriel shrugged, feeling a little as though he were in the witness box. It may have been the environment that brought out Douglas' legalistic side, but he struggled not to be unsettled by it. "I take my lead from Aquinas on that one," he said quietly. "Agnes has made a statement, a statement that by all accounts and purposes is impossible. There are three obvious possibilities: she is a liar making up a story for who knows what reason; she is mad, imagining a scenario in her disordered mind; thirdly, if she is neither a liar nor a lunatic, it seems to me that we must assume she is telling the truth. The bigger question may be how her story *could* be true."

"That's all very well, Father," Douglas protested, lighting up a cigarette with undue agitation, "but people simply do not disappear. It is perfectly possible she was mistaken. The light was poor—"

"Yes, yes, yes, we have been over that possibility. She is, however, very certain that she saw her mother, and, even in poor light, it is hard to see how she could have failed to notice the presence of a human being at that distance—or failed to notice the absence of one, if you prefer."

"The police think she's mad."

"Has she ever shown any signs of being out of her mind?"

Douglas remained poker-faced, as he would have done in court, but he seemed to realise he was on dangerous ground and busied himself putting the cigarette case away. "Not entirely, but—no, mad is a little strong. A bit away with the fairies sometimes, it must be said, and rather nervy, but it was difficult not to grow up a bundle of nerves in our house. There's quite a difference between that and being crazy enough to think one has seen a person who could not have been there."

"Has Agnes ever knowingly lied then? That is a much stronger possibility, if you'll forgive my asking the question."

Douglas went very quiet, always a hopeful sign in Gabriel's opinion that the truth was about to come out. "I hope you don't think me rude, Father, but I'm really not sure this is any of your business."

Gabriel looked fixedly at him. "If none of this is my business, then why did you invite me to your house this morning? It is quite obvious to me that neither of you has much love for your mother, and I suspect she never gave you any reason. Nevertheless, she has a right to justice, and she will never get that if we cannot work out what happened to her in the first place."

"You are not the police, Father."

"Precisely, but it is just possible that the police already believe Agnes is involved with all this. They clearly do not believe her story any more than you do, which is hardly a good starting point in a police investigation. If they believe her to be a false witness, it is only a small step to viewing her as a suspect. If Agnes has ever told tall stories before, I think this would be the time to admit it."

Douglas took out another cigarette and used the dwindling stub of the first to light it. Gabriel detested the smell of cigarette smoke, but he saw that acrid, dirty little curl of smoke slowly polluting the room as the key to getting an honest answer out of Douglas. "I'm only hesitating, Father, because I still do not know all these years later whether she really was lying. It was such a very long time ago; she was only twelve years old at the time. It seems unjust to rake over it now. Would you like to be judged by something you did in childhood?"

"No, I should not like to be judged. But I might accept that the information had to be revealed. You know I will not judge Agnes ill, whatever you tell me. It strikes me that she has been rather hurt by life."

"You know, I hadn't thought of it in all these years until you asked me that question," he mused, and Gabriel could not help noticing his hand trembling, "but I still have no idea if it was a lie at all. You see, she went missing. It was soon after the telegram arrived to say that our father had been killed at Dunkirk. It was a terrible time; Mother was beside herself with grief, but she could never show weakness in front of anybody, and it came out as anger. Neither of us could breathe without her pouncing on us; it was terribly frightening."

"I'm so sorry. How old were you?"

"I was fifteen. Too young to be called up at that stage but desperate to go and fight. Then Agnes disappeared. She went off to play on her own at first light. I suppose she was not sleeping very well at the time because she was upset about Father and went out before I was up. Mother was not very concerned to begin with: we were both used to running wild, and it was almost a relief for Mother to have us out of the house. But when Agnes didn't appear for breakfast or for lunch, Mother became anxious. You see, Agnes hadn't taken any food out with her, so Mother at least expected her to come home to eat, but there was no sign of her. By three o'clock, Mother was beginning to panic. I have never seen her so terrified. We split forces and went round the town looking for her, asking shopkeepers if they had seen her. I went as far as Dr Whitehead's house because I knew Agnes was friendly with his daughter, and down to the Miltons' place, but they had not seen her either. Then suddenly, at dusk—and at that time of year sunset came late—she suddenly arrived at the door."

"Did she explain what had happened?"

"No, that was the frightening thing. She put on this dreamy act as though she honestly did not understand why there was a problem. She kept saying, over and over again, 'But I've only been a couple of hours; why are you so upset?' Mother was shaking her, demanding she tell her where she'd been, but she kept insisting she didn't know. Even I became impatient after a while. It was absurd."

"Had you any suspicion about where she had been?"

"No, none at all. The queerest thing about it is that no one had seen her. No one had any idea where she might be. For nearly twelve hours she really did seem to have disappeared off the face of the earth, and even she claimed she had no idea where she'd been. Mother became angrier and angrier; she shouted, threatened to do anything to her if she wouldn't talk, but Aggie wouldn't tell her anything, though she's normally hopeless at keeping secrets. The next thing, Mother was throwing her about the room; one thing led to another; it all became very ugly. But Agnes still wouldn't say where she'd been."

"Was your mother often violent?"

Douglas stared down at his desk, surrounded by the spectres of his worst childhood memory: his mother shouting as she dragged Agnes into her study and the door slamming and his sister's high-pitched screams as she resisted having a confession beaten out of her. He remembered the days of waiting and the messages of hope on the wireless that victory would be snatched from the jaws of disaster and the tales of brave Englishmen sailing in that glorious flotilla of fishing boats and yachts and dinghies to bring the boys home. But not his father. Not his father.

"Douglas?"

Douglas could not look up. "I don't think I can recall her ever hitting me. Not once. She never needed to. Mother was usually very calm about the whole thing. Very cold and calculating. If either of us put a toe out of line, we'd get a disapproving look, and then she would tell us what we had done wrong and what punishment we had incurred, rather the way she would have behaved at school. She was quite keen on locking us up when we misbehaved; she knew we hated being cooped up."

"But on that occasion, she was frightened and angry."

"Yes. I had never seen her so out of control before. I can still hear Agnes screaming through the locked door, but she didn't tell her anything. She screamed and screamed. If we had lived in the middle of town, I think the police would have come to the door, but no one could hear. If Dr Whitehead had not arrived when he did, I'm really not sure what would have happened."

Gabriel started. "What brought Dr Whitehead to your house? It was hardly on his way anywhere."

"He knew Agnes was missing, of course; he was worried and came to see if she had been found. She made a lot of people worry that day. He heard the commotion and helped me force open the study door. The terrible thing is, when Dr Whitehead carried Agnes upstairs to her room, I felt angry with *her*. I kept thinking, 'Why on earth didn't she just tell the truth? Why let Mother do that to her?' Mother had a right to know where Agnes had been; we'd all been worried sick. I could not understand at the time how she could be so stubborn. It seemed unkind to keep lying like that, over and over again, saying she didn't know where she'd been when she was the only person who could have known."

73

"Did she know you were angry with her?"

Douglas shook his head. "I hope not. I felt guilty about it later. It took her weeks to recover, and, in some ways, she never did. Agnes was very quiet, very on edge after that."

Gabriel sat in silence for a long time, a response that only made Douglas the more agitated, and Gabriel watched the young man light up yet another cigarette, his hands shaking with the effort. "You know you have nothing to be ashamed of. You are ashamed, aren't you?"

Douglas ran a hand across his face, staring up into the corner of the room the way people sometimes do when they are trying to focus their minds. "I felt angry with myself afterwards for feeling angry with Agnes, but at fifteen, all I could think of was how stupid she had been, going off and scaring everyone half to death, then provoking our mother into attacking her like that. Afterwards, I wished I'd been a man and defended her. Whatever it was she had done, nothing excuses what Mother did to her. She drew blood. Dr Whitehead was appalled."

"What do you think she had done?"

"Agnes?" Douglas threw up his arms. "Can it really matter now, Father? I'm not sure I should have mentioned it at all. You can see what I mean when I say I'm not sure she was lying. The saddest part of it is, I doubt she was up to anything very naughty. She was never a naughty girl. At most, it was some silly mischief that would have earned her a rap on the knuckles and bed without supper, but perhaps in her mind it was more important than that. She may have imagined she'd done something very wicked and Mother would never forgive her. The only other possibility, I suppose, is that she really couldn't remember."

"Amnesia? Concussion?"

"It's plausible, surely?" Douglas sounded a little flustered, a professional man being drawn on a subject about which he knew he was ignorant. "Perhaps she suffered some accident while she was out playing, had a nasty fall and hit her head. Maybe a heavy branch dropped on her? I don't know, she certainly behaved like someone with concussion, and Dr Whitehead thought it was probably that. That was what we told everyone anyway. It would certainly explain her confusion."

Gabriel stood up slowly, patting Douglas' arm to indicate that he need not get up to see him out. "Thank you, Douglas, that has been most helpful. Now I suppose I should leave you in peace." Douglas looked stonily through the smoke, and Gabriel knew he was itching for his guest to leave so that he could take out his hip flask. "You should go home," suggested Gabriel, picking up his hat and drifting to the door. "You're not doing yourself any good burning the midnight oil. Who knows? There may still be some innocent explanation for all of this."

Douglas stood up out of sheer force of habit. "Father, you don't really believe that, do you?"

Gabriel shook his head wearily. "I'm sorry, I don't like to give up hope until I have to, but I think you should prepare yourself for the worst, if you haven't already. There is some very great evil at work here, and I don't mean the ghost of a man who never existed."

"It's all right, Father, I will go home," promised Douglas, holding open the door for him. "I'm being a coward holing myself up here."

"Thank you, I hate to think of Agnes all alone out there.

If she really didn't have anything to do with it, she may well be in danger now. She has disappeared before."

You have disappeared before, Agnes, thought Gabriel, as he walked slowly along the eerily silent high street. *Why were you returned, and who returned you? And if you came back alive, why am I so certain your mother never will? Why do I know that she is already dead?*

6

Was it merely a coincidence that two inhabitants of the same household disappeared without a trace? Gabriel wondered over breakfast the following morning. Although the disappearances occurred years apart, Gabriel could not help but think they were related.

The savage way in which Enid Jennings had dealt with her daughter did not, unfortunately, surprise him at all. Very few examples of human cruelty could shock a man at his stage of life, and he could easily imagine how a woman like Enid might respond if she were frightened, angry and repeatedly thwarted by a child from whom she demanded absolute obedience and deference.

But Agnes' disappearance for twelve hours—that did surprise him. If Douglas had said that Agnes had provoked an angry scene for anything else—wandering off with a friend, stealing apples from a farmer's orchard—he would have been surprised that she had had the freedom of spirit to do such a thing, but it would have told him very little of any use. Her disappearance, on the other hand . . . Still mulling things over, Gabriel put on his shoes, picked up his breviary and crossed the courtyard into the church to say his morning prayers.

Fr Foley had finished saying Mass only fifteen minutes before, and the church felt warmer than it would otherwise have done, even though it was already virtually empty. An old man knelt near the back, praying the Rosary; nearer the front, at the side chapel to Saint Patrick, a child dropped a coin into the box with a clink and began the fiddly task of lighting one of the penny candles and spiking it onto the metal rack beneath the statute of the Apostle of Ireland.

The Lady Chapel was at the front of the church, in the left-hand corner, separated from the sanctuary by a thin wall of plaster. Gabriel had an enduring fondness for this little corner of the church. There were always fresh flowers and a few candles burning, but it also contained the one truly beautiful piece of art in the entire church, a vast oil painting bequeathed to the parish by a local couple who had lost four of their sons in the Great War. The painting was a reproduction of a much older Madonna and child; both Mary and Jesus wore Renaissance dress, but Mary looked as young as she would have been, with a round, girlish face full of wonder; her hair beneath its white veil was thick and dark, setting off her tawny skin tones and huge brown eyes. Unlike so many depictions of the Blessed Mother, she did not look Italian or French or Anglo-Saxon; she was a young Jewish girl holding a chubby, rosy-cheeked toddler with one plump arm held up in blessing and the other pressing gently against his mother's shoulder as though protecting her. There was an easy domesticity about the painting that enchanted Gabriel, and he often found himself looking up from the words in his book to gaze at the picture.

As Gabriel reached the Lady Chapel, he realised that there was someone there already, and he stepped a little more quietly so as not to disturb her. It always felt like an invasion of privacy to interrupt a person at prayer, and he knew who it was. Her white mantilla partially concealed her face, but as he knelt on the steps of the sanctuary and looked sideways at her, he could see Agnes deep in thought. He suspected that she had spent much of Mass in tears and was only just beginning to compose herself, but she looked up at the picture with all the agony of a person mourning the loss of a mother or, in Agnes' case, mourning the mother she had never had.

Gabriel contemplated going over to her and offering some words of comfort, but he knew she could only want to be left alone, so he walked slowly out of the church, steeling himself against the cold as he stepped outside.

The cold was to be the least of his problems. Dr Whitehead was standing on the steps talking to Detective Inspector Applegate. They broke off the conversation as soon as they saw him, but Gabriel knew at once what had happened. "Good morning, Inspector," greeted Gabriel warily. "I wish I could say what a pleasure it is to see you again, but I doubt you are here for a happy reason. Has she been found?"

Applegate nodded in acknowledgement. Like most members of the police force, he had very little time for amateur detectives. He was still smarting from his last encounter with Gabriel, but this was not the time for old grievances to emerge. "The drowned body of Enid Jennings was discovered at first light by anglers down at Port Shaston. I have been transferred here to take charge of the murder enquiry."

Gabriel could not hide his confusion. "Forgive me, but I thought Port Shaston was—"

"Yes, about fifty miles away, but her body may have been

adrift for several days. The river has powerful currents at the best of times, but heavy rain at this time of year will have hastened it along, no doubt."

"It's a nasty business," Dr Whitehead put in, as though not wishing to be forgotten. "Coming so close to Christmas as well. I don't know how Aggie and Douglas are going to take this."

"I presume Agnes does not know yet," asked Gabriel. "She looks terrible, but—"

"We are on our way in to break the news now, Father," Applegate explained. "Dr Whitehead here is an old friend of the family, and he has agreed to accompany me. He fears Agnes may require his assistance when she hears the news."

"If he needs me to—"

"No thank you, Father. I'm sure we'll manage. I've had to break bad news once or twice before."

Gabriel watched the two men enter the church, Dr Whitehead walking ramrod straight, Applegate hunched very slightly about the shoulders like an inconveniently tall man used to stooping to speak to others. He felt grateful for Dr Whitehead's presence in Agnes' hour of need. Applegate might be an excellent policeman, but Gabriel thought that he would rather have heard bad news from virtually anyone else. He walked with undue slowness across the courtyard to the front door of the presbytery, listening for any indication that the news had been broken, but there was deathly silence from within the church.

Inside the presbytery, Fr Foley was eating breakfast without much enthusiasm.

"They've found the body," said Gabriel, grateful to have someone to whom he could pass the news.

"Enid Jennings?"

"Yes, fifty miles away, at Port Shaston." Fr Foley immediately put down his toast and crossed himself, making Gabriel realise that that should have been his first reaction too. A woman was dead—she almost certainly died a sudden, violent, unprovided-for death—and rather than pray for her soul, his first thought had been: *But how on earth had she died there? How on earth did she die like that?* He was still caught up in the madness of it all as Fr Foley crossed himself a second time, indicating that he had finished praying. "It doesn't make any sense, Father," sighed Gabriel, sitting down at the table. "It all makes even less sense now."

"I'm not sure murder ever makes a great deal of sense," remarked Fr Foley, getting up to find his friend a cup and saucer. "Would you like some tea?"

"I mean the whole thing makes no sense. Agnes really couldn't have seen her mother from that window. Even if she did not die at Port Shaston, she cannot possibly have died anywhere near that house. When Agnes claimed to have seen her, she might already have been dead."

Fr Foley made no response until he had placed Gabriel's tea in front of him. "If you'll forgive me for saying so, you do seem to be unreasonably determined to prove that Agnes is telling the truth here. I know that she told you she saw her mother disappear under her nose—the whole town is talking about her story—but you've had only her word for it from the first. She was obviously wrong, I'm afraid."

Gabriel shook his head. "You'll think me frightfully bloody-minded, but you wouldn't say that if you had heard her."

Fr Foley gave a reproachful smile. "You'd best listen to

81

me before you go on some wild goose chase. I've known Agnes for years, and she was always a bit touched. You know perfectly well that old battleaxes do not just vanish into thin air, unless you think Enid Jennings bilocated at the hour of her death?"

"When you put it like that, it all sounds so ridiculous."

"Indeed."

"It's no good, Father, I am going to have to see Agnes," declared Gabriel, stepping towards the door with the air of a man snatching a bottle of whiskey from the back of the cupboard after promising faithfully to kick the habit. His long black coat and his hat hung on the coat stand, inviting him to step outside again. "I shall run mad if I can't work this one out, and I have a nasty feeling Inspector Applegate has more plans this morning than breaking bad news to the poor girl. A constable could have performed that task."

"You think she'll be arrested?"

Gabriel sighed. "It will hardly be the first time Applegate has locked up the wrong person."

By the time Gabriel had left the house again, Applegate was standing alone outside the church, scribbling into a notebook. Gabriel could just make out the figures of Dr Whitehead and Agnes disappearing down the street, Dr Whitehead supporting Agnes as she dragged her feet every step of the way. Applegate glanced up at Gabriel. "I thought you wouldn't be able to resist a good gawp," he said, smiling thinly. "Before you ask, you nosy parker, the doctor is taking Agnes back to his house so she doesn't have to go back to that mausoleum she lives in. She's under strict instructions not to leave his house without informing me."

"Is she going to stay there for the time being? It would make sense."

"No," answered Applegate, tipping his hat more to close the conversation than as a gesture of respect. "I fully expect her to spend some time enjoying His Majesty's hospitality before the day is out, but I'm not quite ready to make an arrest this minute."

Gabriel froze, watching as Applegate turned away and began the walk back to the police station. "You can't mean that?" he demanded, hurrying after him. "Surely you don't believe she's mad as well, do you?"

Applegate did not ease his pace for a moment. "Oh no, Father, I don't believe she's mad in the slightest. I *know* that her curious little story is a very clever distraction."

"How so? How can you possibly—"

Applegate had an unpleasant habit, Gabriel remembered, of stopping abruptly and wheeling round to glare at his opponent when he had begun to tire of the conversation. "Really, Father, whatever else was it going to be? You never really believed she watched a woman vanish in a puff of smoke, did you?"

"I don't recall there being any puffs of smoke," Gabriel retorted, finding Applegate's tone as jarring as ever. "It does seem a rather peculiar story to invent. I'm inclined to believe that when a story is too improbable to be true, it is quite likely to be true. There are so many eminently more sensible things she could have said."

Applegate rolled his eyes, quickening his pace with the precise intention of discomfiting Gabriel. "A woman claims to have seen her mother walking along a path when she may already have been dead. Enid Jennings could not have gone anywhere near that house; she was murdered miles away. Yes, the story is ludicrous, but it's not my problem if the suspect is a bad liar."

"Do we have a cause of death?"

Applegate seemed relieved at the change of subject. "Not confirmed yet, but she drowned."

"I don't suppose there's any chance it was an accident, perhaps? I always like to give humanity the benefit of the doubt."

"Don't bother, Father. I stopped doing that years ago. I don't need the coroner's report; I can smell foul play a mile away."

"I suppose . . ."

Applegate smiled with what was almost fondness. "If you found the smoking gun in a killer's hand, you would try to find some way it could have arrived there by accident and fired itself. What else could have happened? An elderly widow vanishes into thin air, reappears in some scenic spot miles away, takes a little stroll along the water's edge and gets swept to her death by a freak wave?"

Gabriel shrugged, miserably. "It is a puzzle indeed, Inspector."

7

Gabriel wondered—as he desperately tried to be interested in the blow-by-blow account of his companion's burst appendix and the complexities of having it removed in the nick of time—if it were a sin to be bored witless by pastoral work such as this. He hardly ever enjoyed the over-seventies lunch club, which met every week, but it was one of his less exacting duties, and some of the men and women who turned up regularly had very interesting stories. They had a certain gravitas by nature of being Victorians—proper Victorians, unlike a Johnny-come-lately like him—individuals who remembered the old queen's jubilee and Jack the Ripper and Gordon of Khartoum.

It was just that the puzzle of a disappearing woman was preying on his mind, and he was desperate to find a reason to stroll over to Dr Whitehead's house and talk to Agnes before Applegate got it into his head to arrest her. He could sense that the inspector was desperate to drag her down to the station—to appear to be on the ball, if nothing else—and once she had been arrested and formally charged, it would be more difficult to speak with her alone. Worse than that, when a person was accused in such a formal way, he tended to close up and refuse to trust anyone, even a person trying to help him. All in all, it would be much easier if he could spend five minutes with her in the safety and welcome of the good doctor's house.

Gabriel was suddenly aware of the silence and realised the old man had stopped talking and was awaiting some kind of response. "Yes," he said emphatically and hoped that this was what was demanded of him.

"Splendid!" said old Mr Cork. "That's very kind of you, Father, really most decent. I know how busy you are, but with all your coming and going I was sure you would find time somehow or other."

Gabriel blenched. He could have just agreed to lead a pilgrimage to Walsingham, to sell himself into slavery to raise money for the roof-repair fund or to hear the man's confession. He had no idea what was so splendid about his answer. "Yes," he said again, fishing for more information to put him out of his misery.

"It will save me a walk," continued Mr Cork, "and Lord knows I was slow enough before the operation. Now this church is about as far as I can manage, and then it's only about fifty yards from my front door. Did I ever tell you I used to run cross-country for the county? Hard to imagine it now, eh?"

Mr Cork had indeed told Gabriel on many occasions that he had been a champion cross-country runner once, but Gabriel was still none the wiser as to the task he had agreed to perform, other than that he seemed to have agreed to go on some errand, which was a good deal better than a life of servitude. Well, that depended, of course, on where on earth he was supposed to be going. "Indeed," said Gabriel desperately.

"Righto, let me pass this to you now then, or I'll no doubt forget all about it." He rummaged in his jacket pocket and pulled out a white envelope. "If you could drop it into the hospital this afternoon, that would be splendid. I'd post it, but it's already a little late as it is."

Gabriel suppressed a groan. It would have been too simple for the letter to require delivery to the cottage hospital at the other end of town. Mr Cork meant the much bigger hospital ten miles away along hilly, winding roads. He suspected that Mr Cork—a farmhand in his younger days and as strong as an ox—would once have thought nothing of walking that distance, but he probably imagined that Gabriel could drive a car and had a special supply of petrol coupons. "Yes," said Gabriel, putting the letter away. "Consider it delivered."

As soon as Gabriel had said a prayer of thanksgiving, he got up to leave, citing urgent parish business (it was certainly urgent and definitely had something to do with the parish). He felt a pang of guilt at leaving two or three worthy ladies to do all the clearing away; not to mention the sad gaggle of hangers-on who could not face dispersing to their solitary homes just yet and were prolonging the lunch by standing in a little group chatting.

I really ought to invest in a bicycle, thought Gabriel, as he marched off in the direction of the doctor's house. He could not drive, and with the persisting petrol shortages, it felt wrong to run a car unless he absolutely had to. In any case, there was something about being seen walking about the town that he hoped made him approachable. People knew that they could walk alongside him and engage him in conversation if they needed to speak with him without having to make a formal appointment. Gabriel had used the tactic to great effect when he was at the abbey, but today he walked with his head down and only just acknowledged the waves and greetings of passersby as he went.

He knew perfectly well it would inconvenience the doctor to be handed a letter to deliver at a hospital he barely ever attended, but Dr Whitehead did have a car, and Gabriel convinced himself that he was discharging his duty to Mr Cork by handing it to the doctor instead of going ten miles out of his way to shorten the arrival of a letter by twenty-four hours or so. He suspected the missive was just a thank-you letter to the hospital staff who had looked after him, since Mr Cork had managed to get ill on his one journey away from home in months and had been treated there. The request to deliver the letter, however, did at least give Gabriel a tenuous reason to visit Dr Whitehead that did not directly involve Agnes.

～

"Good afternoon, Father," greeted Mrs Gilbert, Dr Whitehead's frighteningly efficient housekeeper. "You must have come to visit Agnes."

Gabriel felt his shoulders drooping as he stepped inside the house and removed his hat and coat. "Actually, I was hoping to catch Dr Whitehead if he's not too busy."

Mrs Gilbert shook her head in a mildly irritating way. "He's in the surgery; he won't be finished for at least another couple of hours. If you're unwell, of course . . ."

"No, it's quite all right. I simply had a message to pass on to him from one of my parishioners." Gabriel pressed

Mr Cork's letter into Mrs Gilbert's reluctant hand. "Perhaps you could pass this on to Dr Whitehead when you get the chance? The parishioner asked for it to be delivered to the hospital, but I'm afraid I don't have a car." He gave a judicious pause as Mrs Gilbert glanced suspiciously at the address before slipping the envelope into her apron pocket. "Since I'm here, it would be a good idea for me to see Agnes. How is she? I was terribly worried about the state she was in this morning."

"Well, it's hardly a surprise that the poor girl's in a state," replied Mrs Gilbert, leading him upstairs. She was a tall woman with the build of a cottage loaf, which caused her to walk with an odd, swinging gait as though struggling to transfer her weight from one foot to the other. Gabriel could hear the suppressed wail of a woman weeping before they had reached the landing. "Between you and me," Mrs Gilbert added, pausing for breath at the top of the stairs, "this is bad even for Agnes. The doctor's just given her a sedative, but it hasn't taken effect yet." She rapped sharply on the door and opened it a little before calling, "Agnes, dear, I have a visitor for you. Someone to cheer you up."

With that, Mrs Gilbert pushed the door open and signalled to Gabriel to go in without entering herself. "Thank you," he said, stepping past her. "I shan't be long."

"You won't have long," answered Mrs Gilbert bluntly. "If the doctor's done his job properly, Agnes should be fast asleep in about ten minutes. Whatever you've got to say, you'd better make it quick."

Gabriel stood in the doorway and let his eyes become accustomed to the dim light. Mrs Gilbert had closed the floral curtains, which darkened the room considerably. It was a comfortable spare room, well aired and spotlessly clean with a homely feel to it, thanks to the soft furnishings and yellow and white striped wallpaper. With a little more light, it might even be quite cheerful. Agnes lay curled up on one side in the bed, half buried in the layers of pastel bedclothes.

"Agnes."

Agnes turned in Gabriel's direction at the sound of her name being gently called. She had always had a pale complexion, but the prolonged, perhaps quite hysterical crying had turned her face an alarming shade of scarlet, the skin mottled and damp like that of a woman battling a severe fever. "Have you come to hear my confession?" She whimpered, turning away again, which was almost a relief.

Gabriel moved cautiously towards her bedside and sat down in the armchair by the wall, which put enough distance between them to prevent her from becoming alarmed but left them close enough to be able to speak without the risk of being overheard. "I came to see how you were bearing up," said Gabriel, "but if you wish me to hear your confession—"

Agnes let out a groan that startled him, and for a moment he was unsure what it meant. "It's far too late for that, Father," she said.

"You know that's not true, Agnes, why don't you let me—"

"Don't!" she snapped, as he opened his bag to take out his stole. "I don't even know if I *want* to be forgiven. This is a judgement, Father."

Gabriel dropped his bag at his feet and attempted to make eye contact with her, but Agnes had closed her eyes. "Agnes,

I know you've been given drugs to help you to sleep, and any moment now you will fall asleep. Please tell me what you mean by that. We might not get another chance to speak."

Agnes crushed the edges of the bedclothes in her fists. "I detested her, Father. I wanted her to disappear. I wanted her dead, and now she is. What sort of person hates her own mother enough to want her dead?"

Gabriel drew a deep breath. "Agnes, nobody dies because someone simply wants him to."

"I might have killed her with my own bare hands, Father!" she shouted suddenly, but her words, though very loud, had a rasping tone to them that warned him the drugs were indeed taking effect.

"Agnes . . ."

"She came to haunt me. She knew it was because I hated her; the moment she died she must have come to haunt me!"

"Agnes, my dear, now you really are being irrational," said Gabriel. "When you saw your mother at the window, she was alive. There is no other explanation; you saw your mother alive. How on earth she got to the place where she was killed is a mystery we are going to have to work out together. But the figure you saw on that path was a living, breathing woman."

Agnes glanced at Gabriel beneath lowered, swollen eyelids. "You do believe me then, Father? You do believe I saw her?"

"Naturally. That is what I needed you to know, because the next few days are going to be very hard for you. I thought it would be easier for you to hang on to your convictions if you knew you had an ally."

"Thank you." Agnes looked up at him as though anticipating a question. "Was that all you came to tell me?"

"Of course," answered Gabriel, standing up to leave. "Now don't fight the urge to sleep. Let it come; you need to rest."

Gabriel hesitated in the doorway, listening as Agnes' breathing became slower and more regular; then he stepped out onto the landing into Inspector Applegate's waiting arms.

"You might have made your presence known!" hissed Gabriel, directing Applegate towards the stairs. "It's pretty bad form to go eavesdropping on a conversation like that."

"You weren't hearing her confession, were you?" asked Applegate dryly.

"As a matter of fact, no, I wasn't. Nor have you any right to ask me that."

"Just checking that nothing I heard was protected by the seal, that's all."

Gabriel winced. "And what exactly did you hear?"

"Practically nothing, I'm afraid. You two don't half mumble. Nothing of any use except—" he cleared his throat theatrically. " 'I might have killed her with my own bare hands!' "

"Might!" enunciated Gabriel. "She said *might*! That's a different matter altogether. Surely you don't really believe that counts as evidence?"

"Not evidence, no. Something resembling an admission of guilt perhaps."

"Oh, don't be ridiculous! The girl was distressed, nothing more. She has just lost her mother." Gabriel became aware of Dr Whitehead standing at the foot of the stairs, listening solicitously to the argument.

"Quite right, Father," Dr Whitehead put in. "May I ask what you were doing, Inspector? I said I required five minutes to get ready. Was there any particular reason for you to wander upstairs?"

Inspector Applegate looked unusually embarrassed. "Forgive me, Doctor, but I had more than one reason to call on you today, I'm afraid. I need to take Agnes Jennings in for questioning."

"Out of the question," answered Dr Whitehead with the calm authority of a man used to deference. "I have just given Agnes a sedative. She will be of no earthly use to anyone for at least eight hours." Dr Whitehead turned to Gabriel. "I have agreed to identify the body on behalf of the family." He glanced back at Applegate with a dismissive nod. "It's quite all right, Inspector, I know my own way to Port Shaston—I assume she's in the mortuary at Queen Alexandra's?"

"She is."

"Well then," said Dr Whitehead, picking up his hat as though closing the conversation, "I shall drive there directly. I do not require an escort."

Gabriel felt a guilty sense of schadenfreude, watching Applegate hesitating to argue with the doctor even though it meant losing face. The case was hopeless. Applegate gave a slight bow and saw himself out of the house. He took three or four steps in the direction of the gate, beyond which his car was no doubt parked, before adding: "If you could please come and see me as soon as you have finished at the mortuary, I would be most obliged."

Dr Whitehead gave the smile he reserved for agitated male patients desperately attempting to cling to their dignity in embarrassing situations. "I shall not fail to do so, Inspector," he promised.

As soon as he was sure Applegate was definitely out of earshot this time, Gabriel turned to Dr Whitehead. "I hope this doesn't sound presumptuous, Doctor, but I wonder if I might accompany you to the mortuary?"

Dr Whitehead looked a little taken aback. "Why ever would you want to do that, Father?" he asked. "You barely knew her."

"Well, she was a Catholic, albeit devoutly lapsed. I should like to anoint her if it's all the same to you."

Dr Whitehead shrugged his shoulders amiably. "I don't suppose it can matter much now. As it happens, I should like to talk to you anyway. Hop in, we'll drive over together."

Gabriel could not help feeling a boyish sense of excitement to be in the passenger seat of Dr Whitehead's splendid little motor. The doctor was as careful a driver as Gabriel had imagined he would be, navigating sharp corners and uneven surfaces with the ease of a man who has travelled these roads for many years. Within minutes, the cottages of the town gave way to the breathtaking beauty of the Wiltshire countryside, and Gabriel began to relax. The sight of the expansive green fields, divided here and there by brackish hedgerows and sad, bare trees, brought him in mind of the abbey and his brothers there, snug inside secure stone walls.

"Dear me, not a good sign at all," joked Dr Whitehead, indicating a field full of Friesian cows, almost all of which were lying down in the damp, long grass. "We shall have rain."

"Thank you for looking after Agnes," said Gabriel. "With Douglas so busy, I'm sure it's a relief to him to know that she's being cared for."

"It's no trouble at all, Father," Dr Whitehead replied. "She's practically family. Best friends with my daughter for years. I can't pretend I'm not extremely worried about her. That was rather why I wanted to speak with you. That lout Applegate thinks she did it. That was why he came to speak with me earlier today. It had nothing to do with identifying the body; I volunteered to do that myself."

"I see. Why?"

"Hmm?"

"Why are you identifying the body? Shouldn't that be Douglas? He's the next of kin."

Dr Whitehead sighed. "Do you know how Douglas' father died?"

"Killed at Dunkirk, wasn't he?"

"Yes, in a manner of speaking. He drowned on the way home. The fishing vessel carrying him capsized. Applegate said Enid Jennings had drowned, and I thought Douglas really oughtn't to be viewing bloated corpses. He appears far stronger than his sister, but he's been a nervous wreck since the war. I wanted to spare him the misery."

"I suppose he must have felt the need to be strong when his father died. Man of the house and everything."

"Indeed. I'm sorry you never knew Harry Jennings. The family was destroyed without him. Never really recovered; Agnes seemed to come off worst."

"Would you mind if I asked a delicate question?" asked Gabriel, after a judicious pause.

"I've a feeling you'll ask it anyway," answered Dr Whitehead wryly. "Well?"

"In your professional opinion, how sane would you say Agnes is?"

Dr Whitehead smiled reassuringly. "Father, she is as sane as you or I, but she has been through a great deal more than you know, and I'm afraid it takes its toll on a person. I have given her story some thought, as it happens."

"Yes?"

"Well, it occurred to me that people have disappeared before in these parts—without there being an abductor or a killer, I mean. I daresay Douglas has told you about the time Agnes went missing, but there was another occasion when I was a boy."

"A disappearance?"

"Yes. It sprang to mind as soon as Agnes told me what had happened. A farmer was out walking with his six-year-old son, a little boy called Archie. They were running across a common, not far out of town, and the child ran ahead and disappeared. The father thought nothing of it, since the ground is so uneven in these parts. He assumed the little one had just stepped into a dip in the land; but he walked and walked, and there was no sign of Archie anywhere. There was nothing but grass and little hills all around; no trees, no hedgerows where he could be hiding, but he was gone."

"What on earth happened?"

"Well, fortunately Archie's father was a sensible chap; he knew there must be some reasonable explanation. He ran back to his farm, gathered together his labourers and they went back to the place where Archie had disappeared. They formed a column and walked slowly across the ground, looking for any way in which Archie could have vanished from sight. Finally, the men stumbled upon a fissure in the ground, completely concealed by the long grass. It was too narrow for a man to fall through and would be noticeable only if one stepped into it, but of course it was wide enough for a small child, and that was what had happened. When they parted the long grass and shone a torch down there, there was Archie wedged in between the two walls of earth. He'd knocked himself unconscious as he fell, which was why he hadn't called for help. The men got him out and carried him home. Sometime later, he came round with no recollection of what had happened and no ill effects. Just an amusing story to tell in the pub years later."

"How extraordinary! Is that what happened to Agnes?"

Dr Whitehead gave him a sidelong glance, and Gabriel had the sense that he was encroaching upon forbidden territory. "I'm afraid not, Father. No one knows what really happened to Agnes that day—even her, apparently. The point is, there are many underground caverns in this part of the world, but people generally know about them. Cheddar Gorge, Wookey Hole. The adventurous go exploring down there. And if one were to fall through a gap in the earth as Archie did, one wouldn't get out without help. Agnes would not have got out without assistance, and why on earth would anyone rescue a child like that and then just leave her to wander home alone? Someone would have said something."

"I suppose so. And presumably she would have been filthy."

"Precisely. I wondered in Mrs Jennings' case, wondered

just for a moment about it, simply because of that story from long ago. But the fact is, Agnes' story simply doesn't make sense. If there were a hole in the ground large enough to swallow a grown woman, it would be difficult to hide. She may well not have even been alive when Agnes claims to have seen her. And if she was, how the devil did she end up where she was found, when the Jennings' cottage is so far away from anything, even water?"

Gabriel sighed, trying not to sound dissatisfied. "It feels like the problem of a reliable girl versus an impossible situation. My every instinct tells me she's telling the truth."

"I'm not calling her a liar, Father," Dr Whitehead assured him. "She's a good girl; make no mistake about that. The fact is, she was petrified of her mother and with good reason. I know one should not speak ill of the dead, but you cannot begin to imagine what a monstrous tyrant that woman was. One does not have to be mad for one's mind to play tricks on itself from time to time. I suspect that all that happened was that Agnes was anxious about her mother's arrival because she had had a friend round for lunch whom she knew her mother despised; she was so caught up imagining her mother's appearance that, for a moment, she truly thought she had seen her. A moment later, the madness passed."

"It's plausible," admitted Gabriel. "I'm afraid I'm more at home with the mysteries of the human soul than the mind."

Dr Whitehead smiled indulgently. "And so you should be, Father. But speaking as a doctor, I honestly cannot think of another explanation, and I won't have the police harassing her. Agnes is like a daughter to me; I won't see her come to harm over this."

"I understand."

"And incidentally, Father, you are a hopeless liar," added Dr Whitehead cheerfully. "I do know my catechism, and I know perfectly well you priests do not anoint the dead."

Gabriel felt himself blushing. "Well, I'm glad you know your catechism," he tried, embarrassed. "Look here, I'm not trying to incriminate Agnes. I too believe her to be innocent, but I shan't be able to help her without evidence. I need only a quick glance at the body, I swear, and I'll leave you in peace."

"That's quite all right, Father. Take as long as you need."

Gabriel sat back in the passenger seat and distracted himself with looking out at the avenue of beech trees they were driving through. *Dr Whitehead is no fool*, he thought, *and he wanted me to know it.*

8

Gabriel had very rarely entered a mortuary; his business was largely with the living. His last sight of a person tended to be in those final sacred minutes at the deathbed, before the person's cadaver was put through the indignity of being transferred, labelled and, in some cases, submitted to a post-mortem. Everything about the ghastly building rankled with him. In this unnatural time between death and the solemn farewell of the Requiem, a body became a piece of meat to be looked at or stored away. There was something so municipal about it all, the chill ambient temperature; the cold, spartan room in which the body lay; the indifference of the mortuary attendant, who had somehow found himself stuck with a job he could never speak about at dinner parties.

A young man with the face of a medieval hangman led Gabriel and Dr Whitehead to the shrouded figure, gave them both a perfunctory glance as though attempting to acknowledge the distressing nature of their task, then took hold of the sheet and pulled it back. To Gabriel's mortification, he found himself closing his eyes as the sheet fluttered back to avoid the first shock of seeing a dead body and opening them two or three seconds later to find Dr Whitehead already shaking his head. "That's her all right," he said calmly. "That is Enid Jennings."

The mortuary attendant nodded and stepped back. "Would you like a few minutes?" he asked.

"Yes please. We shan't be long. The priest here would like to pay his respects—in private."

The attendant nodded again, turned on his heel and left. Dr Whitehead glanced towards the door as it swung shut before turning back to Gabriel, "I could hardly contain my shock," he half whispered. "This is not what I expected at all!"

Gabriel moved towards the body and took a closer look. It was definitely Enid Jennings; her face was unmistakable even in death. Gabriel had often found that as soon as someone died, the person's skin seemed to unfold as the muscles relaxed, giving a look of peace and tranquillity, almost youthfulness in the old ones as the lines of anxiety smoothed out. Everyone looked like an innocent in death, except apparently Enid Jennings, who still managed to have a slight scowl on her face. It was as though she maintained an intense disapproval of the world and everyone in it, all the more so now that it held no place for her. "What a terrible thing," he said without thinking, "to die with all that anger."

"Father, I wasn't referring to her facial expression. Look at her!" Gabriel looked again, wincing slightly as Dr Whitehead removed the sheet altogether so that he could get a full view of her body. Enid Jennings' clothes had turned something like the colour of dishwater from being soaked in the muddy river for hours; she wore no jewellery except her wedding band—an almost sentimental gesture for a hard-bitten widow. Her hair had become unpinned as she was dragged along the river, and the hat she had almost certainly been wearing must have disappeared without trace in the water. It felt strange to see her without a hat, almost intrusive. She had lost a shoe as well, and her naked foot had a badly grazed heel from scraping along the stony riverbed. "Father, can't you see?" called a voice from far away.

"Her fingernails are a terrible mess," commented Gabriel, looking from one of her hands to the other. Both sets of nails were ragged and had dirt buried deeply underneath them. "Poor grooming for a woman as fastidious as Mrs Jennings."

"What are you wittering away about, Father?" came the impatient response. "The point is, she's not bloated."

Gabriel winced again. Dr Whitehead was right, of course. "She didn't drown," Gabriel stated matter-of-factly. "She was dead before she landed in the water. The river's so fast-flowing at the moment, her body must have been carried along by the powerful current and tangled up in something before it could sink." He glanced up at Dr Whitehead for support. "So what was the cause of death?"

"The postmortem will tell us that," said Dr Whitehead finally, respectfully recovering the body with the sheet. "The only thing I can say with any certainty is that she didn't drown. We may not even be looking at murder here." Dr Whitehead shook his head again. It was the first time Gabriel had ever seen him looking unsettled or even uncertain of himself, but he clearly did not know how to proceed. "Let's get out of here, Father," he said finally, making for the door without looking back to see if his companion were following. "I don't know what to make of any of this now."

Back in the car, the two men sat in silence as Dr Whitehead slipped the key into the ignition and brought the engine to life after three or four attempts. It was Gabriel who spoke first. "May I look at that list of her personal effects?" he asked, if nothing else to divert the conversation from the enormous elephant in the vehicle.

Dr Whitehead slipped his hand into his pocket and pulled out a piece of paper folded twice. "Nothing much to read there, Father," he remarked, releasing the hand brake and sending them cruising down the road. "I should think the contents of Enid Jennings' salvaged handbag will prove to be the least mysterious part of all of this."

"Possibly," said Gabriel, casting his eye down a list of predictably mundane objects: a black leather purse containing a water-damaged ten-shilling note and a punched train ticket, a door key, a yellow pocket comb, a white cotton handkerchief and a fragment of water-damaged paper, possibly a shopping list. "I like to have as much information as possible."

"I'm not given to existential experiences, Father," remarked Dr Whitehead, "but I feel as though I've walked into some strange dream. I suppose at least there's a possibility now that the woman did not meet a violent end, even if the mystery has thickened a little. There's quite some comfort in that, I suppose."

"But the mystery has thickened."

Dr Whitehead studied the road ahead. "The mystery of what happened to Enid Jennings, perhaps, but if we go by the premise that Agnes was mistaken when she looked out of the window, the whole situation feels a little more straightforward. Mrs Jennings made a decision to go somewhere else after she had spent time with her sister. Perhaps she had arranged to meet someone. I can't think of anyone offhand, but a woman that age would not necessarily choose to share her plans with her children. She was fiercely independent. Exactly where she went or what happened next we do not know as yet, but at least there might be some sanity to the whole incident."

But I can't accept the premise, thought Gabriel glumly. *I shall be written off as a madman, but I know Agnes saw something . . .*

~

Next morning, Gabriel was woken by his alarm clock to find his bedroom in complete darkness. When he pulled back the curtains, he was greeted by a misty haze on the other side of the pane of glass, so thick and impenetrable that he could see nothing at all out the window. He was used to the way in which fog could roll down across the fields unpredictably, spreading confusion amongst all those who were forced to go out and find their way whatever the weather, but he also knew it was likely to lift very quickly before much of the morning was gone. He closed the curtains and began the daily ritual of washing and dressing, reciting briefly at the foot of the bed: "O Jesus, through the most pure Heart of Mary, I offer thee the prayers, work, sufferings and joys of this day, for all the intentions of thy Divine Heart in the Holy Mass."

Gabriel wandered downstairs to find Fr Foley hanging up his coat and hat, having just returned from saying the early morning Mass. "I found this hand-delivered note addressed to you on the doormat," said Fr Foley as he handed Gabriel an envelope.

"Someone was out early," Gabriel said, tearing it open without going in search of his paper knife.

"Or very late," suggested Fr Foley. "But it would have had to be very late indeed. I'm afraid I was a little restless in the hour or two after I retired, and I came downstairs. There was certainly no note there then."

"It's from Douglas Jennings," Gabriel explained. "I suspect he did put it through the door very late; he's a night owl at the best of times. I doubt if he even went home last night. Probably slept on someone's sofa rather than face that house. And Agnes is still staying with the Whiteheads. . . He writes that he wants me to visit him at his office at eight o'clock, before anyone else arrives. Is that all right?"

"You don't need my permission," said Fr Foley, but his normally jocular face had adopted a more serious expression than Gabriel was used to seeing. "Are you sure you want to go alone?"

Gabriel raised an eyebrow. "Do you think I oughtn't?"

"No, of course not. I'm sorry, please ignore a mad old man. Douglas Jennings is a decent sort. I suppose this whole business has been rather distressing, that's all. They say people are locking their doors at night. Never thought I'd see that here."

"It's quite all right, Father," said Gabriel, tearing up the letter and turning away to throw it in the bin. "He may know that I went to view the body with Dr Whitehead and want some information without risking anyone else overhearing. I can quite understand that."

"I daresay."

"Well, you know what it's like. The silence after a disaster like this is almost the worst. No arrests, no leads, no certainty at all as to what actually happened, and the police homing in on the one person who is least likely to have anything to do with it."

Fr Foley gave him a wistful look. "Dom Gabriel, you're a fool if you convince yourself that anyone is innocent in all this. Both of those Jennings children had reason enough to do away with her, and half the town would have cheered them on."

"That's a dreadful thing to say!" Gabriel retorted. Fr Foley used a mockingly formal tone with him only when he was being deadly serious, and Gabriel felt a misdirected sense of betrayal. The old man ought to see things the same way as Gabriel, even if no one else did.

"Don't take it the wrong way," Fr Foley protested, aware of how callous he had sounded. "You know how I feel about the taking of innocent life. But you know, it's a very sad state of affairs when a woman dies under suspicious circumstances and not one person, not *one* offers Mass for her or even expresses regret at her passing. I can't think of another occasion in the long, long years I have served this parish when a person was quite so hated that there was no one, even in his own family, who was sorry to see him go."

"There's her sister," suggested Gabriel desperately.

"Possibly," Fr Foley conceded, "but she has hardly rushed to the assistance of her niece and nephew, has she? I doubt you'll see any sign of her, except perhaps at the trial. Assuming there ever is a trial."

The sight of the light shining from Douglas Jennings' office window reassured Gabriel as he walked the last few yards through the soupy darkness towards Mr Pitman's solicitors' office. The fog was so bad that no one was out who could avoid it and those who were out did not acknowledge him, the need to concentrate on moving safely and slowly being stronger than courtesy. Any place that gave a little heat and light at this time of year felt safe and welcoming on such a miserable morning.

Gabriel had to wait several minutes at the door whilst Douglas came down the stairs to let him in, and, when he did, Gabriel found the interior of Douglas' office almost as impenetrably smoky as the outside. "Fumigating your conscience, are you?" coughed Gabriel. He could already feel his eyes stinging as he found his way to a chair. "How long have you been here?"

"Since five, Father," announced Douglas, sitting back in his seat. The smoke had begun to dissipate as soon as the door was opened, and Gabriel looked intently at the dispiriting sight before him: Douglas sat with his shoulders drooped and his head slumped forward, looking every bit like a convicted criminal awaiting the footsteps of the hangman. "All right, Father, as you can see, I have been here all night. I couldn't face going home to an empty house, and when Dr Whitehead's lovely wife offered me a bed for the night yesterday evening, I was too ashamed to accept. I couldn't have her thinking I needed coddling as well."

"You should not have refused her kindness," said Gabriel. "It might have done you good to be under the same roof as Agnes. You might have got yourself a halfway decent night's sleep for a start. You look terrible."

"Thanks."

"Terrible" was putting it mildly. Douglas was a wreck, and he doubted anyone else would fail to notice. His clothes wore the crumpled look one might expect on the body of a man who has not changed or washed in well over twenty-four hours; he was not a swarthy man, but his face showed an obvious need for a shave; his eyes—always the clearest indicator of a man's state—bore the ravages of sleep deprivation, smoking and far too much to drink. "You'd better tidy yourself up a little before anyone else arrives," suggested Gabriel. "You're in no fit state to see your clients."

"It's quite all right, Father," said Douglas dismissively. "It shan't be the first time I have had to stay in the office overnight. I have a sponge bag in the cloakroom for just such an emergency." He inhaled the acrid air without enthusiasm. "Now, I don't have much time, and I need to talk to you."

"Of course."

"I'm having Agnes committed to an asylum."

Gabriel took a moment to register what he had said, and his shocked response was so delayed that it caused Douglas to jump to his feet as though he expected a fight. "What? On what grounds? She's no danger to anyone; she's just very upset!"

"Father, it's for her own safety! Dr Whitehead telephoned me yesterday to say that the police had turned up again."

"I know. I saw Applegate there."

"The very same. He was so desperate to take Agnes in for questioning that when Dr Whitehead told them yesterday afternoon that she would be out for the count for at least eight hours, they took him at his word. Applegate turned up with a constable at exactly nine o'clock at night." Gabriel groaned; he could just imagine Applegate being as pedantic as that, all the more so if he felt aggrieved at having been sent on his way earlier by an officious member of the medical profession. "Fortunately, she was so bleary and it was so late that Dr Whitehead was able to persuade them that it was unfair to take her in then. Well, he was quite right, of course. She would have been in no fit state to be interviewed, and I would not have allowed her to speak with the police without the presence of a solicitor. Myself, if necessary."

"I see." Gabriel shifted in his chair. "You know I can't stop you, and I understand that you want to protect your sister, but it seems a rather drastic step to have her locked up."

"It's all right, Father," said Douglas defensively. "It's not one of these ghastly Victorian asylums: it's a perfectly nice private clinic not very far from here. Greenford's. It has only recently opened. You know, that place that used to belong to the Malmesbury family." Gabriel shook his head. It was yet another part of the local geography he had failed to notice. "It is a perfectly respectable place, lots of lovely gardens, and the rooms are clean and—and Dr Whitehead spoke very highly of the doctors. To be frank, he's arranging everything."

"Was it his idea?" asked Gabriel quietly.

"No, as a matter of fact. It was mine, but I knew he would be able to help with all his contacts. It won't even be for very long. Just long enough for everything to blow over." Gabriel could see Douglas out of the corner of his eye, struggling desperately with the temptation to pick up his cigarette case. "Dr Whitehead told me about what he saw at the mortuary," he continued. "If he's right, it may be that there was no crime at all. In which case, life may settle down quite soon."

"Couldn't she stay on with the Whiteheads? They seem perfectly happy to have her."

Douglas sighed. "They are very decent people, but Dr Whitehead is a busy man, and his wife is busy running his surgery and looking after her own family. Even if it weren't for the police breathing down her neck, Agnes needs someone who can keep a close eye on her. She may do something desperate."

Gabriel sat in silence, pondering what Douglas had said. It was certainly true that Agnes was in a dangerous state, distressed, frightened, requiring frequent sedation, and a well-run clinic would take care of her needs better than anyone else. However, he had a natural discomfort about establishments like that. He had seen so many young men after the first war committed to institutions simply because there was nowhere else for them to go and no one who really knew how to take care of these nervy, angry, depressed former soldiers. Gabriel knew that it was all too easy for a person to be admitted to one of these places for the convenience of others and never leave. He might become so accustomed to institutional life that he would be unable to cope after a while with the uncertainties and fluidity of the outside world, or he might simply be forgotten. Relatives could live their lives in peace and comfort themselves with the thought that their loved one was well cared for, ignoring the nagging feeling that they had got a problem off their hands by telling themselves over and over that it was the best possible solution.

"I will not lie to you and say I entirely agree with this," said Gabriel at last, "but you have clearly made your decision, and I trust Dr Whitehead's judgement that he will not allow her to fester there unnecessarily. What was the real reason you called me this morning?"

Douglas threw open his hands in mock surprise. "I wanted to discuss my sister's welfare, Father. Is there anything wrong with that?"

"No, there isn't. But there was never anything to discuss. You have already made plans, and you simply wanted my support—which I cannot honestly give. What was the real reason you called for me this morning?"

Douglas leant back in his chair, raising his eyes to heaven. The repeated question at least had the effect of waking him up a little. "Very well, Father. I wanted to see you because Dr Whitehead told me that he had given you a list of my mother's personal effects. I wondered if I might look at it or if you could remember what was listed there."

Gabriel smiled and held up the folded paper. "As a matter of fact, I was rather hoping to ask you about this myself. What is your reason for wanting the list?"

Douglas shook his head a little too readily. "It wasn't morbid curiosity, if that is what you think. It's just that she always carried a penknife on her. It was my father's. It was found in his pocket after he died, and she treated it almost like a relic. If they recovered it, I should like to have it if at all possible, once the case is closed . . ." he trailed off. "Look here, it may seem a petty detail under the circumstances, but I have very few mementoes of my father. My mother destroyed virtually everything after he died."

"Why would she do that?" asked Gabriel automatically, but his mind was preoccupied by a more pressing question.

"She wasn't thinking; it happens. I had rescued quite a few bits and pieces she had wanted to throw away. I kept them under my bed mostly, but one day she found them and became very angry. I always thought she felt jealous of how important to me he had been. She smashed absolutely everything, tore up photographs. I think she regretted it afterwards, which is why she hung on to the penknife so religiously. She could not put all those things back together again."

Gabriel dropped the list onto the desk between them like a token of goodwill. "It seems to me, Douglas, that on the rare occasions your mother lost control of herself, she was exceptionally dangerous."

"Terrifying, Father."

"Dangerous enough perhaps to cause another person to fear for his safety."

Douglas narrowed his eyes, sensing that he was being taken down a path he did not wish to walk. "You may surmise that much from what happened to Agnes. Yes. I could imagine being frightened enough of her to lash out, if that is what you mean." Douglas snatched up the list and opened it quickly.

"I'm very sorry, Douglas," said Gabriel gently, noting his deepening frown, "but I'm afraid there is no penknife listed there. Are you absolutely sure she left with it?"

Douglas nodded, visibly deflated. "She would not have left without it, and I would have found it in the house by now if she had. I daresay it must have fallen out somewhere. It was heavier than the other things she carried."

Gabriel glanced at Douglas, who really did look like a despondent little boy who had lost some imagined treasure. "I'm so sorry to ask this of you, Douglas," he said warily, "but there was something I wanted to ask you quite urgently. It's about Agnes. I wouldn't ask if I didn't think it might help her."

Douglas shook his head, pushing away the paper as though it had personally let him down. "No need to apologise. What is it?"

"Could you cast your mind back, please, to the day Agnes went missing."

Douglas gave a groan of exasperation. "Oh Father, it was years ago! Why do you keep going back to that? Agnes turned up safe and sound. It's all very mysterious, but she wasn't hurt, by whatever happened anyway. My mother contributed that part of it."

"Are you sure she wasn't hurt?" Gabriel pressed him. "Was she very dirty, for example?"

Douglas shook his head absently. "No, not that I recall. I would have remembered. Dishevelled yes, and I dare say she'd been cleaner, but I don't remember that she was dirty. Why?"

"Only a theory you've exploded, that's all," Gabriel smiled, "but it's best to rule out all possibilities. Besides being dishevelled, though, are you sure she didn't have any injuries? You know, grazes, for example? Anything that might suggest a fall?"

Douglas threw him a withering look. "If she had, my mother destroyed all the evidence fairly quickly. You've no idea what a child looks like when she's been attacked like that; she looked as though she'd been flayed alive. If she'd hurt herself before . . ."

"Yes?" Gabriel knew that Douglas was weighing up an idea in his mind, without quite knowing whether to share it. "It's all right, say it even if it doesn't appear to make any sense."

"It's not that, Father, it was just rather a small thing really," Douglas explained. "Well, if I remember rightly, when Dr Whitehead was cleaning her up, he pointed to some bruises on her arms. I remember him asking where they'd come from and thinking it was such a stupid question. She'd just been beaten to within an inch of her life. Where else could she have got them? I think I said so. 'Same place as everything else, Doctor,' or something regrettable like that."

"And what did he say?"

"I think he said, 'I very much doubt it' or something. After that, the conversation took a different turn, and that was the end of it."

Gabriel was suddenly animated, which had the effect of unnerving Douglas. He actually backed away a couple of steps. "It's all right, Douglas, but this is important. The bruises, you said they were on her arms. Could you demonstrate?"

"Well . . ." Douglas splayed the fingers of one hand and pressed them across the opposite arm, just above the elbow. "About here, I suppose."

"Both sides?"

"I don't know, she was lying down, I couldn't see her other arm from where I was standing." Douglas looked searchingly Gabriel. "If the bruises were already there, my

115

mother didn't put them there. It would have been too soon. You knew there was something there, didn't you? That's the sort of trick a barrister would play, only asking the question when he knows the answer."

"I wasn't trying to trick you, Douglas, I promise," Gabriel assured him, "but I did have a suspicion. And I'm sorry about that penknife. Who knows? It may still turn up."

9

Gabriel knew now where he had to go next. Douglas had confirmed the niggling suspicion that had kept him awake at night, and there was only one person he could think of who could tell him what he needed to hear: Abbot Ambrose, the fount of all knowledge. Gabriel's only difficulty was that the abbey was too far away to walk to, and a bus would take hours, winding its way through endless villages between here and his destination. But Dr Whitehead had been foolish enough to offer to help, and in a car he could be there in under half an hour. The doctor would not even have to stay if he did not want to, though Gabriel was sure he would be given a welcome and a cup of tea if he wished. He planned to ask the abbot if Brother Gerard could drive him back when he had finished.

It was not homesickness, Gabriel told himself, as he rushed back to the presbytery to get through his morning chores as quickly as humanly possible; not homesickness as such, but a tiny part of him felt that he was returning to the abbey for reassurance, much as a child might run home to his parents for consolation after a difficult day at school. It was not the first time in his life that he had had this powerful sense that he was walking very slowly in the right direction, albeit in the dark and with every passerby screaming at him to turn around. All the same, the events of the past few days had made him feel lonely. He missed the opportunity to share ideas with sympathetic friends, even friends who might finish the conversation by telling him he was going barking mad.

What with one thing and another, it was half past eleven before Gabriel had some time to himself again, and he made a mad dash to leave rather than face the horror of lunchtime at the presbytery and one of Dorothy's delightful offerings. Fr Foley's itinerant housekeeper had never been the most talented of cooks, Gabriel suspected, but the limitations of rationing had shrunk her repertoire to dishes almost exclusively involving corned beef, cabbage, potato and swede, a root vegetable for which he had developed a particular loathing. That said, he thought it would be bad form to turn up at the Whiteheads' at the moment Mrs Whitehead was serving lunch because she would undoubtedly want to set a place at the table for him and the food she had prepared would have to stretch to satisfy another adult appetite. He could tell her he was expected to eat at the abbey; honour and etiquette would be satisfied.

Gabriel was still some distance from the doctor's house when he saw a figure up ahead, only just distinguishable in the poor light as a woman in what appeared to be a long coat and a sharp winter hat with little in the way of a brim. She was walking very quickly, virtually running, and Gabriel eventually gave up trying to catch up with her and called out: "Pamela?"

The figure stopped in her tracks and turned to face him.

He had been right. It was Pamela Milton, out of breath and more flustered than he would ever have expected to see her. "Father?"

Gabriel closed the gap between them as quickly as he could. "I dare say I'm easy to see from far away," he said lightly.

"Yes," she answered with a half smile, "You look like Count Dracula. I suppose you've heard the news then?"

Gabriel felt his heart sink; of course he hadn't. He had been stuck in the parish office all morning, but he knew what must have happened, or Pamela would not be running to the scene. "Agnes?"

"Yes, I thought that must be the reason we were heading in the same direction. I'm trying to reach the doctor's house before they take her away."

Gabriel touched her arm in what had been intended as a comforting gesture, but Pamela turned away and continued walking, allowing him the privilege of trotting along beside her. "You know, it may be for the best, and it won't be for very long. Douglas said the place is very nice."

Pamela stopped again, looking at him as though he were a blithering idiot. "What are you talking about, man? I was at the bookshop with my daughter when someone came in and said that the police were going to arrest Agnes. Apparently, that clot of a PC Plod has decided that Agnes is an accessory to murder. She is supposed to have made up the story of seeing her mother through the window to detract attention from what was really going on. You know, causing the police to keep the search local, diversion tactics, blah blah blah, the usual nonsense. The idea being that the killer, whoever it is supposed to have been, could dump the body and have plenty of time to cover his tracks. It's like something out of an Agatha Christie."

They continued walking. "But I thought Enid Jennings had been seen leaving the railway station? If that's the case, the police must be able to ascertain that she came back to the town even if she didn't return home. If so, it suggests—"

"Yes, yes, yes, Father, I catch the drift. The problem is, as George—Mr Smithson—was kind enough to point out earlier, it will be almost as difficult to prove that Mrs Jennings arrived at the railway station as it will be to prove that Agnes saw her spectre through the window. There are plenty of old ladies in big hats getting on and off trains. They'll just argue that the stationmaster saw someone else getting off the train. Mrs Jennings was hardly the most sociable old crone in the town; she would not have stooped low enough to talk to anyone. Any good legal counsel would demolish a witness who claimed to have seen her."

"What a mess" was all Gabriel could think of saying, and he immediately wished he hadn't bothered. He thought: *You are giving this far too much thought, Pamela. What are you playing at?*

"That's the understatement of the decade!" snapped Pamela. "I just wish to goodness she hadn't been alone. If we'd stayed a little longer or Douglas hadn't felt the need to push off . . . I thought it a little rude anyway at the time."

"Well, it was certainly very convenient of Douglas to disappear like that," mused Gabriel aloud, another comment he immediately regretted.

Pamela went quiet, ostensibly to catch her breath, but as though aware that Gabriel was reading her thoughts, she said quickly, "Fortunately, he went to a public place where people knew him."

"Indeed. There would have been only about half an hour either side of his arrival at the pub in which his movements were unaccounted for. Forgive me. Why not forget I said that?"

"Consider it forgotten, Father. I don't suppose Applegate has asked you where you were at four o'clock on that afternoon, has he?"

"Touché. Oh dear." Gabriel came to a halt like an exhausted marathon runner taking a few pathetic final steps. "This does not look promising at all."

Inspector Applegate's car was parked awkwardly in front of the handsome facade of the Whiteheads' house. Gabriel and Pamela could hear what sounded like a violent argument, and they both rushed to the door, Pamela arriving shortly before Gabriel.

Inspector Applegate and Mrs Gilbert were standing in the hall in the middle of a blazing row. Applegate's normally dour complexion was flushed with unprofessional anger, whilst Mrs Gilbert wore the look of a woman whose territory has been invaded by the Visigoths. "It's no good threatening me, *Inspector*," she hissed at him, as though the word "inspector" were an expletive. "I had nothing to do with the decision. Mr Jennings thought it would be better for her."

"Did you drive her to that so-called clinic?" thundered Applegate. "I'll have you arrested for obstructing the police."

"Inspector—" Gabriel began, but the interjection sounded no stronger than a whisper in the context of two raised voices.

"Of course I didn't, you imbecile; I can't drive!"

"The doctor then?"

"He's been busy with patients all morning."

"Inspector, look behind you," said Gabriel, but the effect was disastrous. Reminded of a pantomime scene, Pamela burst out laughing, causing both Applegate and Mrs Gilbert to turn and look at them. Gabriel looked apologetically at Applegate. "I really would look behind you."

Standing in the doorway leading to the adjoining surgery stood a thin, white-haired woman and a much taller, younger woman with soft blonde curls; they were evidently mother and daughter. In her arms, the young woman held a baby who was whining softly and looked as if he had been woken up by the noise. "What do you think you're doing?" demanded the white-haired woman in a surprisingly strong tone. "How dare you come into my house and interrogate my housekeeper like this for half the town to hear. We could hear you shouting from the waiting room."

"I'm sorry, Mrs Whitehead," said Applegate, "but I've come here on serious business. I'm afraid I need to arrest Agnes Jennings, and I gather that she's been spirited away to some loony bin or other."

"I'm not sure I know what you mean by that term," answered Mrs Whitehead, stepping determinedly into the centre of the room. Gabriel marvelled at how such a physically unimposing person could so easily take control of the situation. They had all gone quiet, including Applegate, who for the first time looked a little awkward. "Would you care to remove your hat?" she asked, diminishing Applegate even further; he fumbled to remedy the oversight. "Now, for your information, Agnes was not spirited anywhere. I drove her to the clinic myself over an hour ago. If you are going to arrest anyone for getting in your way, I'm afraid you'll have to arrest me. Then, you can drive over to Greenford's and arrest Agnes in her sickbed."

Gabriel glanced from face to face and noticed that the four women were all glaring at Applegate in accusation, a detail not lost on Applegate either. He drew a deep breath, spreading his hands in front of him as though in self-defence. "Now look, Mrs Whitehead, Agnes is not sick, she's hiding—"

"My husband thinks otherwise," answered Mrs Whitehead, coldly. "At which medical school did you train, Inspector?"

Applegate flinched with the final undermining remark he was apparently capable of enduring; he turned his back and pushed past Gabriel and Pamela in his determination to remove himself from the advancing female army. Gabriel nodded in Mrs Whitehead's direction before following Applegate outside.

"Inspector?" he called, but Applegate already had his hand on the gate and the constable had got out of the car to come and speak with him. "Inspector, please wait a moment."

Applegate turned on him, unleashing the pent-up fury of the past ten minutes. "You knew they were taking her away, didn't you?" He roared. "Admit it, you were in on the whole plot!"

"I very much doubt it is a plot," tried Gabriel, "but if you really think she's an accessory—"

"I don't know who told you that. I wasn't about to arrest Agnes for being an accessory to murder; the charge *is* murder." Gabriel opened his mouth to respond, but Applegate cut him off. "We all swallowed the idea that she was in that house all along, didn't we? But who can vouch for her after Dr Milton and the others left? She has no alibi at all from three o'clock that afternoon until the following day. Oh, don't pretend to be shocked!"

"Her brother can vouch that he found her in a distressed state near the house that evening. I know there are still some unaccounted-for hours, but even so—"

"Laudable for a man to give a false alibi for his own flesh and blood. I suspect we might both do the same. And if you think I believe his story, you must think I believe in Father Christmas. I'd wager she got that blow to the face from her mother trying to defend herself."

"I'm sure Douglas is an honest man; he's a man of the law."

Applegate gave an appalling, sneering laugh. "What sweet naivety, Father! No lawyer has ever lied to the police."

"Inspector—"

"Look here," said Applegate with the tone of a man who is closing a conversation once and for all. "I don't know who it was who said that doctors are the most dangerous men in the state, but they're not. Lawyers are. They're clever; they know the workings of the law; they know how to cover their tracks."

"Inspector, what evidence can you possibly have? Enid Jennings died at Port Shaston. It's not even clear if she met a violent death at all."

"What?"

Gabriel instinctively took a step back from Applegate's piercing gaze. "It looks as though she didn't drown," he said lamely. A sudden image came into his mind of one of those propaganda posters depicting two women chatting together over a cup of tea with Adolf Hitler in the background listening in: *Careless talk costs lives.*

"The information I have been given is that she drowned," said Applegate emphatically, and there was only the slightest threat in there somewhere. "The results of the postmortem are not yet available." Gabriel looked away, unwilling to volunteer any further information. "I'll thank you not to interfere any further," said Applegate in little more than a whisper. Gabriel suspected that the occupants of the house were watching them from the doorway, and he struggled not to reveal anything through his body language. "I wouldn't want to have to lock you up as well."

"On what grounds?"

"I don't know, Father," whispered Applegate, looking him coldly in the eye. "Rumours can spread quite quickly in a little place like this, even false ones."

Gabriel swallowed hard as Applegate opened the gate and walked with the constable to his car. He watched as the car drove away, aware of the queasy feeling creeping through his gut. He took so long to come to himself that he eventually became aware of a hand on his shoulder. "Father, whatever is the matter?" asked Pamela. "What did he say to you?"

Gabriel was conscious of the determined hand of another person taking him by the arm and leading him back into the haven of the Whitehead house. "It's nothing," he said, but Mrs Whitehead was immediately fussing, telling Mrs Gilbert to fetch some brandy from the cabinet. He was vaguely aware of the sound of a baby screaming upstairs and realised where the other woman had gone. "I'm quite all right," he said quietly. He was almost more shocked at his own clumsy handling of the situation than Applegate's threat.

"You're nothing of the sort," said Mrs Whitehead, leading him into the kitchen where he was immediately assailed by the glorious aroma of bread baking. "I hope you don't think it improper of me to bring you into the kitchen, Father, but it's the warmest room of the house in winter and your hands are freezing." He sat in a surprisingly comfortable wooden chair by the stove and watched her opening a large tin. "I'm just glad Agnes is safe for the moment. Evil little brute. And didn't even have the manners to remove his hat. Did you see the state of his boots?"

Gabriel shrugged miserably. "I'm not sure I did, Mrs Whitehead. Don't worry about getting cake out for me; it'll spoil my appetite."

Mrs Whitehead gave an indulgent smile and handed him a generous slice of fruitcake. "Excuse me if I can't give you a larger slice," she explained, "but you know what paraffin can do to the constitution. I have found ways to produce plenty of food, but sugar and butter remain elusive. There now, let me see where Mrs Gilbert has got to with that brandy."

"Really, I—" Mrs Gilbert was pressing the glass into his hand, and he had no energy to resist her kindness.

"Threatened you, did he?" asked Mrs Whitehead, pulling up a chair and siting down opposite him. She had the kind, cheerful face of a woman who has led a largely contented and sheltered life at the heart of a happy home. She had no pretensions to great beauty but was the sort of person one could warm to effortlessly. "Don't take any notice, Father. The police don't know what they're doing, and one of my husband's chums has told me that you are good at puzzles."

"I'm not sure I'm making a very good job of this one," Gabriel admitted. The cake was more of a treat than the brandy, and he felt himself warming up immediately as he sank his teeth into the soft, crumbly sweetness. "You are very fond of Agnes?" he asked between mouthfuls.

"She's practically family, Father," said Mrs Whitehead. "There were times after her poor father died when she virtually lived here. It was difficult at home. For all her reputation as a battleaxe, Enid Jennings—God rest her soul—couldn't cope at all after her husband's death. Douglas was old enough to look after himself, for the most part, and then, of course, he was called up as soon as he turned eighteen, but Agnes needed somewhere to turn."

"It was very good of you."

"It was nothing," Mrs Whitehead assured him. "She's a dear little thing, always was. She and Therese were like sisters for a time."

Gabriel was finding it awkward to talk and eat tidily at the same time. He endeavoured to keep his hostess talking. "Are they still close?"

Mrs Whitehead's smile faded. "They drifted apart when they started growing up. It happens with girls, always falling in and out of friendships. They're on cordial enough terms now that they're both grown." She hesitated. "Forgive me, Father, but did you come to the house to see Agnes again?"

"I'm afraid I didn't," admitted Gabriel, letting Mrs Whitehead remove his empty plate with only the smallest regret.

"Though it's because I'm trying to help Agnes that I wanted to ask a favour."

"Of course. What is it?"

Gabriel cringed with the English embarrassment of asking for anything. "I need to go to my abbey. There's someone there I wish to consult about this matter. It's just that it's rather a distance and the buses are dreadful . . ."

"I'll run you over as soon as I've laid out the lunch things," she said with a smile.

~

It is strange the way memory can play tricks on a man's sense of time passing. As they came into view of the abbey, Gabriel could have believed for a moment that he had been away for only a couple of days. It felt so natural to be there, all the more so after he had clambered out of the car and waved Mrs Whitehead goodbye, finding himself alone in a particular spot where he had once walked every day.

That was the strangeness of it. He had imagined walking along the path to the gates with a lump in his throat, feeling his eyes misting over with the joy of returning home, but it felt so normal to be home that no emotion touched him at all. He simply rang the bell, a little regretfully because he realised that he had mistimed his visit. The delay caused by his altercation with Applegate and subsequent chat with Mrs Whitehead had meant that they had left the house much later than he had hoped and lunch would be long over. On the bright side, however, it was a time of recreation now, which might make it a little easier for him to speak with the abbot alone.

Gabriel's only nasty moment came when a young novice opened the door to let him in. He must have entered in the months of Gabriel's absence, because Gabriel could not place his face at all. "Good afternoon," said Gabriel, dismissing from his mind the image he had had of rapturous greetings from Gerard or Dominic. "I'm here to see the abbot."

"Do you have an appointment?" asked the young man.

Gabriel tried hard not to flinch. "No, but I'm sure he'll see me."

The young man looked extremely doubtful but noted his clerical dress and let him in anyway. "Whom shall I say is calling?"

"Dom Gabriel," he answered with emphasis. "Please tell him it's urgent."

As they walked up to Abbot Ambrose's room, Gabriel looked around hopefully for a friendly face, but everyone seemed to be hiding. He noticed a familiar fluttering of nerves in his chest as they walked up the stairs and approached the door; it was out of character for Gabriel to be knocking on Abbot Ambrose's door voluntarily and through his mind flashed all the awkward moments, mistakes, complaints and reprimands he had experienced over the years. It was best not to think too hard about such things, but Gabriel was really not sure how Abbot Ambrose would feel about his sudden appearance on an errand he might well regard as frivolous.

Gabriel's fears dissipated as soon as he was escorted into the room. Before his guide could announce him, Abbot Ambrose looked up from his desk and gave a rare smile. "Good Heavens!" he exclaimed, putting down his pen. "Isn't that strange? I was just thinking about you." He turned to the novice. "Thank you."

As soon as they were alone, Gabriel said, "Forgive me for intruding like this without an appointment, but I didn't think it prudent to speak over the telephone."

"The Soviets have not taken over yet," answered Abbot Ambrose dryly, "but sit down anyway. I've heard about this vanishing woman, and I couldn't help fearing you have got yourself caught up in it all."

"It was rather difficult to avoid, I'm afraid," said Gabriel, seating himself awkwardly at the edge of the chair. "It's a small town, and I'm acquainted with most of the suspects. Enid Jennings was a lapsed Catholic, and I'm afraid she's not the vanishing woman anymore either. She's dead; they found the body."

Abbot Ambrose was well versed in the art of being inscrutable, and his face did not flicker before he responded: "What a dreadful business. I'm afraid I rather assumed she was dead, but one always has a little hope that a missing person may return unharmed." He narrowed his eyes in Gabriel's direction. "Don't tell me: the police are baffled, and you have taken it upon yourself to investigate."

"Well yes, the police are baffled, and I'm not getting very far with investigating. I am, however, trying to help a young woman in rather a bad way. That was what I wanted to consult you about."

Abbot Ambrose leant forward. "Go on."

"The dead woman lived with her two adult children in an isolated cottage. The woman's daughter, Agnes, claims that she saw her mother walking up the path to the house when she suddenly disappeared into thin air. No sign of her was found in the vicinity. At first it was treated as a missing-person enquiry—no one really believed the poor girl's story, but Enid Jennings was definitely missing. Then, in case the daughter's claim were not absurd enough, her mother's body was found all the way in Port Shaston. The swollen, fast-flowing river will have dragged the body many miles, but it still doesn't explain how the body came to be anywhere near water in the first place or how Agnes could have seen her mother through the window at around the time or possibly even after the time of death."

Every time Gabriel retold the story, it sounded a little more fanciful, but Abbot Ambrose glanced impassively at his folded hands until Gabriel had stopped talking. "The woman was mistaken about what she saw," suggested Abbot Ambrose. "It was a trick of the lights, the result of an overly fertile imagination. Dare I suggest it might even be a lie?"

"I know, all those possibilities sound quite sane compared with what I'm about to suggest," said Gabriel awkwardly, already anticipating the response he was going to get. "For all sorts of reasons I will not go into at the moment, I'm fairly convinced that Agnes *did* see something out of that window, in fact I'm pretty sure she did see her mother and she saw her mother alive. She's refused to back down, even though she's being labelled a lunatic or even possibly a criminal."

Abbot Ambrose gave the sigh of the worldly wise. "I was once called upon to speak with a perfectly nice gentleman who was convinced that he was Abraham, the patriarch. I tried every possible line of argument to convince him otherwise, but he could not be convinced. He was adamant that he was Abraham and was able to cite all kinds of perfectly logical arguments to back up his claim."

"I know what you mean, Father Abbot," Gabriel conceded, feeling himself shrinking physically at every word, "but there is no other suggestion that Agnes is insane. She is a very troubled young woman, certainly, but besides this story, she shows every sign of being in possession of her mental faculties. It stands to reason that if she is not lying and she is not mad—"

"Yes, thank you, Dom Gabriel," Abbot Ambrose cut in. "I too have read some Aquinas. I assume you have a little hypothesis you wish to share?"

Gabriel sat up as tall as he could. "As a matter of fact, I do. There is one other possibility that keeps coming back into my mind. She might have fallen into an underground cavern—"

The sound that distracted Gabriel began as a wheezing, rasping noise reminiscence of an ancient accordion being played by an amateur musician. Then Abbot Ambrose's cadaverous face cracked open, and he roared with laughter.

"Does it really sound so ridiculous?" asked Gabriel, but he could feel himself reddening with the shame of it. "I know it sounds mad . . ."

"That is because it is entirely barking mad," said Abbot Ambrose, when he had collected himself. "If there were a phenomenon like that practically on the lady's doorstep, it would be very visible and everyone would know about it. The opening would have to be large enough for a grown woman to fall through. And even with heavy rain, it's highly unlikely that a hole that huge would suddenly open up without giving the woman time to escape."

"I wouldn't even have considered the possibility," said Gabriel with the persistence of a man walking through torrential rain only because he is already too drenched to bother seeking shelter, "but her daughter also disappeared years ago, though she came back unhurt. It seems to be too much of a coincidence that two people from the same family should vanish into thin air like that. I cannot help thinking there must be a connection."

Abbot Ambrose's usual funereal countenance had returned. "Now that is a little more interesting," he admitted, which gave Gabriel some hope. "Do you know in which year the girl disappeared?"

"Yes, more or less. Her brother said it was shortly after their father was killed at Dunkirk, which dates it quite clearly." Gabriel waited for the abbot to answer, but he was staring into the far corner, contemplating what he had just heard. "That's why I wondered, since the first disappearance occurred during the early years of the war, when there was still the serious threat of an invasion . . ." He cleared his throat. "Father Abbot, were there manmade underground chambers dug out during the war? There were air-raid shelters of course, but one would not find a structure like that in such a remote area; there were no bombing raids down there, even stray ones. It just occurred to me that a manmade structure would have been built to be invisible, even soundproof. And secret, of course. You see, Agnes wouldn't tell a soul where she'd been when she was recovered, even when her mother became violent. Her brother, Douglas, thought perhaps that she had concussion or something like that, because she was behaving very strangely. I thought that, well—"

"—that if a child were too frightened to tell anyone where she'd been, even under threat of violence, she must have seen something she was never meant to see and could not risk repeating."

"Exactly. And, like her mother, she really did disappear; nobody could find her all day. It's a small town; if she had been out in the open, somebody would have noticed unless she had taken it upon herself to go deep into the country-side."

Abbot Ambrose fell into one of those deep, impenetrable silences Gabriel remembered so well. Gabriel watched as the old man closed his eyes, resting his chin on his hands as he mulled over the problem, thinking through the many possibilities. Gabriel was aware of the distant patter of footsteps on the lower corridor and the rumbling of his empty stomach, which seemed as loud as an earthquake in such a silent place, but he dared not make any attempt at interruption. He had just let his gaze drift over to the leaded window in the far wall, where he could make out a swathe of dank sky and the smallest square of green in the lowest corner, when he heard the sound of Abbot Ambrose sitting up. "I'm afraid there is very little I can do to help you with this, my son," he said slowly, "I'm afraid I was—well, abroad for much of the war and have little knowledge of operations here. If there were a man-made underground structure, a remote area would be the place to hide it, but the presence of a nearby dwelling complicates matters somehow. The likeli-hood of a child stumbling upon something would be quite a risk, I would have thought."

"The cottage is the only one in the area, and I think that

during the early years of the war there were a lot more trees in the way. It would have been much easier to conceal. And someone put a rumour about, something about a marauding ghost. Children were always too frightened to play there."

"The rumour makes me almost more suspicious," he said. "It's just the sort of thing one might say to keep nosy little urchins off one's back. And of course, if there were any noises or other strange movements, a casual passerby might be convinced something frightening was going on and run away. There's no doubt it would have to be extremely carefully concealed, particularly if the police have raked over the area and not found it."

"To be honest, the police did not do much of a job of looking. The body was found miles away, and no one really took Agnes' story seriously from the start. The fact is, though, I really did look, and I couldn't see anything."

Abbot Ambrose tapped his fingertips against the desk one at a time as though silently counting. "It would have to be carefully concealed, but you see, if such a structure were built at all, it would have been built to be completely secret, impossible to see even if a person were looking for it. They know what they're doing. Incidentally, did the young woman claim that her mother vanished under her very nose or was she looking away at the actual moment?"

"She was looking away. It was only for a moment; she heard the kettle whistling."

"Hmm. I would think that by the time she had moved away from the window to the stove, removed the kettle and switched off the gas, and poured water into a teapot, that would give between twenty and thirty seconds. That's not a negligible amount of time."

Gabriel dared to let his spirits rise. "So do you think, perhaps, I might be going the right way with this?"

Abbot Ambrose looked him calmly in the eye. "I think you may, though you could, of course, be completely wrong. If there is any truth in your suspicion, however, I think you should perhaps be cautious about pursuing this any further. These are very deep waters. Everything you have said makes me uneasy."

"I know," said Gabriel. He considered telling the abbot about Applegate's veiled threat and then decided against it.

"I am simply telling you to be careful, that's all. Two disappearances may not be enough for some." With that, Abbot Ambrose seemed to relax, and he looked in Gabriel's direction with what was almost amusement. "Your stomach rumbles so loudly, I could have heard it from the cloister. Why don't I ask Brother Gerard to fetch you something to eat in the refectory?"

Gabriel could hardly hide his relief as he stood up to leave. "Thank you. I am rather hungry." He added hopefully, "Fr Foley is improving slowly."

"I'm delighted to hear it," Abbot Ambrose replied without missing a beat. "Come and visit us again soon, won't you?"

10

"It's not that bad, is it?" asked Brother Gerard, as they hurtled around the corner, the left-hand wheels of the car screeching horribly as they drove too fast through a puddle. "I always thought parish life must be quite a laugh, really," he added when Gabriel failed to respond. "All that freedom. No bells. Never one day the same as the next."

"I'll swap you whenever you like. Ever heard of the grass is always greener?" responded Gabriel, clinging helplessly to the sides of his seat. In Dr Whitehead's car he had felt like a privileged passenger being gently guided through a tour of the Wiltshire countryside; with Gerard behind the wheel of the clapped-out monastic motor, Gabriel was left with the sensation that he was being put through some kind of me-diaeval ordeal to test his faith in the mercy of the Almighty. If he screamed, he had failed.

"Aw, come on, enjoy it while you can. Before you know it, you'll be back. D'ya have a light?"

"Eh? I don't. You know I don't smoke. Anyway, you shouldn't be lighting up when you're driving. You're enough of a motoring nightmare with both hands on the wheel." Gabriel closed his eyes and tried to relax. "I hope you're right, anyway. It's a nice enough parish when people aren't being bumped off all over the place."

"Not that we can throw too many stones in that direction," Gerard reminded him. "That cottage still gives me the heebie-jeebies to this day."

"Yes, I'm sorry I got you caught up in that dreadful business now . . ." he trailed off for a moment before sitting bolt upright as though someone had kicked him in the shins. "That's the problem with all this!" Gabriel almost shouted, causing Gerard to swerve. "There are too many things that don't make sense! Give me a straight case of somebody clobbering somebody else over the head with a spanner, and I'd be perfectly happy!"

"Nicely put from a man of the cloth," squeaked Gerard. "Now I really need a ciggy."

"You know what I mean; I need something to focus on. But as it is, absolutely nothing makes any sense at all. What the girl saw doesn't make any sense; the location of the body doesn't make any sense. Since absolutely everyone hated the victim, with one or two notable exceptions, everyone's a suspect, and pretty much everyone might have had a motive. Come to think of that, it's not even clear that we are talking about a murder, since the cause of death seems so vague and the postmortem results are taking an age to be released. And if we're not talking about murder, then what exactly is the crime we're talking about?"

"Stop! You're making my head swim!" pleaded Gerard mockingly. "I'd forgotten how much talking to you feels like being thrown off a roundabout."

"My head's been swimming from the start, if it's any consolation."

"You know what Father Abbot would say. Write it all down in a long list. Start with the suspects."

"Practically everyone."

"Narrow it down."

"Let's exclude Dr Milton's sweet little girl and the doctor's infant grandchild."

"Well, it's a start. Clues?"

"An eyewitness account that makes no sense, the body of a woman who ought to have drowned but apparently didn't, and a missing shoe that probably means nothing because it would have been dragged off in the water. Missing penknife, equally possibly lost in the water and, since she wasn't knifed, is probably not relevant either. Her fingernails were a bit of a mess, and there are all sorts of reasons that might be the case."

"Anything else?"

Gabriel shuffled in his seat. "Agnes had a nasty injury to her face dating from around the time of her mother's death, but she and her brother say it was an accident."

Gerard took his eyes off the road to stare at him. "How many times has a woman said it was an accident when some bloke's obviously thumped her?"

"Tractor!" shouted Gabriel, giving Gerard just enough time to get the car back on the proper side of the road. The tractor trundled past them like a gigantic, man-eating insect. "I suppose I should say that the victim was overheard arguing with and threatening Dr Milton before she died."

"Sounds as though you're getting somewhere," he said. "Perhaps it's like one of them crazy modern paintings that you have to stare at until your eyes start to water, then suddenly you see what it's meant to be."

139

"Thanks. It's good to talk again."

They were starting to pass rows of houses on either side, and Gabriel noticed Gerard slowing down as they entered the town, a little more aware of the need for safety where there were people about. "Shall I drop you off at the presbytery?" he asked, turning to look at Gabriel again.

"Woman on bike," stated Gabriel, bracing himself whilst Gerard straightened the course again. "Would you mind dropping me off at the bookshop?"

"Please yourself."

"The bookshop is a little farther down the high street, on the left-hand side."

As Gerard pulled over, bumping up onto the curb accidentally as he did so, Gabriel felt a sudden reluctance to let him go. "Are you in a hurry to get back?" he asked hopefully. "I shan't be long in the bookshop. I could get you a cup of tea at the presbytery before you make the journey back. It's a long way to go without any refreshment."

Gerard's boyish face broke into a grin. "It's not far at all, you clot! I'll hardly die of thirst before I get home, and I'd best be back before dark." He noted how deflated Gabriel looked and patted his arm. "Chin up, mate, you'll be back with us before the year's out, driving us all mad."

"I hope you're right. If there's room for me."

Gerard rolled his eyes theatrically. "Don't go taking against Boniface for treating you like a stranger. He's new; he didn't know. Cheerio!"

"Cheerio," he echoed, but Gerard's chirpy words of farewell only sounded sarcastic coming out of Gabriel's mouth. He raised a hand to wave goodbye, but the car was already spluttering away into the distance. Gabriel could feel the wrench of something more than homesickness. He felt rather like the naughty boy of the family who has just paid a visit to his blissfully happy home and been dumped back on the doorstep of his boarding school.

He was relieved when he stepped into the bookshop to find that there were no customers browsing the shelves and no sign of Pamela's child. George Smithson was in the process of repositioning an old rug that appeared to have been rolled up or moved, perhaps for the purposes of cleaning the floor. "No Scottie today?" asked Gabriel, as lightly as he could manage.

George got up from kneeling and dusted down his hands. "Her mother is taking her out to do some Christmas shopping, thank God," he answered, then checked himself. "Please don't misunderstand me. She's a delightful girl, but she was determined today that there was a secret hiding place somewhere in the shop and wouldn't rest until she found it."

"And did she?"

George laughed and shook his head. "Sadly no, but that did not stop her tapping on every floorboard and every wooden panel, looking behind every book and rearranging all the furniture. All the children's books she reads are full of stories of secret tunnels and hidden trapdoors and priest holes, so naturally she imagines that every old building has them. I'm afraid she was disappointed today."

"Unlike little Agnes."

The effect on George was immediate. The affable smile vanished, his body visibly tensed and Gabriel could have been forgiven for thinking that the man grew a few inches in the process. "I think you had better tell me what you mean by that, Father," he said slowly, throwing him the remorseless look of an interrogator. Any doubts Gabriel had had about his latest mad theory evaporated as he met George's glance and held it across the room.

"You know perfectly well what I mean," he answered. "I know what you did to Agnes. You are no more a bookseller than I am Pius the Twelfth. Now why don't you close the shop and we can talk a little more privately."

George strode towards the door without further prompting, pulled the bolt across and flipped the *open* sign to *closed*. He turned back to glare at Gabriel. "If you know as much as you claim to, Father, I wonder that you are brave enough or foolish enough to meet me alone."

"Perhaps foolish," conceded Gabriel, "or maybe just hopeful that you will do the right thing this time."

George regarded him a little longer before giving a nod in the direction of the backroom. "Very well, let's get the kettle on."

Gabriel followed George behind the counter and through a battered interconnecting door that looked as though it hung permanently open. The backroom into which they emerged consisted of a small kitchen area marked out by a square of worn lino on the floor and an L-shaped work surface with a single gas hob on one side next to a sparklingly clean sink. Several newly washed cups stood to attention in a row on the draining board. The other half of the room was an Aladdin's cave of heaving bookshelves, the books stacked in serried ranks by size and colour rather than by author or subject matter; the old rocking chair looked almost insolent in the shabby but spotless room, slouching at a lazy angle between the obedient books and a small, polished table with its lieutenant—a smaller, lower stool—tucked away neatly beside it.

George filled the kettle, took a box of matches out of a drawer and lit the gas ring with a neat little pop before setting the water to boil. "Am I allowed to ask what you have worked out, Father?"

"Well," Gabriel began, perching on the stool. He had some vague sense that he should not make himself too comfortable in the rocking chair in case he had to make a run for it. "Would you be offended by the title 'retired spy'?"

"Yes," said George, mildly. Gabriel noticed that he made no attempt at turning to face him. "Retired makes me sound old, and spying makes me sound—I'm not sure what. I don't feel somehow that it does justice to the occupation. How did you know?"

"Quite a few little details gave it away. Look at this room, for example."

"You've only just walked in here," George pointed out, reaching into a cupboard to take down two white teacups and saucers.

"It confirms everything, that's all. The tidiness of it, the particular way everything is sorted. It speaks of a military man."

"Well, there are plenty of those about. Being a former military man hardly makes me anything else, does it? And I could simply be very tidy."

"Indeed. But then there's your knowledge of languages. You speak fluent French—nothing unusual about that, I suppose—but you are fluent in several languages, aren't you? I noticed the series of books in French and German on a shelf near the counter. If I may say so, there cannot be very much demand for foreign literature in this town, and virtually nobody buying German literature at all. Nor were the books merely part of a collection. There was no sign of dust and the pages were cut, suggesting they had all been read."

Gabriel glanced across the bookshelves, pulling out the collected works of Goethe, only for George to spin round, advance on him and snatch the book out of his hands, replacing it immediately. "I say, do you mind?" George demanded, then took a step back as though conceding a position. "I'm sorry, but I don't altogether like this."

"Then there's your name, of course," Gabriel continued, ignoring the man's discomfort. "George Smithson. It's just a little too generic, only one step away from Smith, the ultimate pseudonym. It made me think that perhaps you had done your work, the war ended and you were sent packing with a modest sum of money and the instruction to live a quiet, anonymous life." Gabriel paused, mentally ticking off the list. "My only question would be, why did you settle in the place where you had served? Surely it would have been better to move somewhere entirely new, where there was no chance of anyone finding you out?"

George was busily opening the tea caddy, a task that seemed to take an inordinately long time. "I was not stationed here long once the threat of invasion had passed, and more importantly I was not raised here," he said. "In this part of the world, that counts for quite a lot. If one settles in a town like this in adult life, one is always regarded as a bit of a foreigner. And there were many people, many men who came and went during the war. No one really took them very seriously, except young ladies, of course, and I was not much of a lothario, even in those days. In my line of war work, one did not allow anyone to come close, especially a woman."

"Keep mum, she's not so dumb," recited Gabriel.

"Exactly. When I was stationed here, I was invisible. No one even knew that our base existed." He placed a brown ceramic teapot, cups and saucers, a milk jug and a sugar bowl—containing virtually no sugar—on the tea tray and carried it over to the table. "Help yourself, Father," he said, sitting down in the rocking chair but with his torso rigidly upright, defeating the point of the thing. "I hope you don't have a sweet tooth; I'm afraid I lent Pamela most of my sugar ration. She's hoarding for Christmas. But then, I will be attending Christmas dinner at her house, so I suppose I should call it an investment rather than a donation."

"Have you told Pamela about Agnes?" asked Gabriel, quietly, and he would have forgiven George for thumping him.

"Why the devil should I?" George scrutinised Gabriel's every move as he poured a little milk into his cup and reached for the teapot. "It was a long time ago, in a very different world. And I would appreciate it if you were not to go talking to her yourself, Father. It would ruin everything."

Gabriel took an inordinate interest in the sight of the cup filling with brown tea before he could summon up the courage to answer. "Mr Smithson, if a woman were not dead and you did not have another child in your care, I should not hesitate to respect your privacy."

"I had nothing to do with Enid Jennings' death," said

George emphatically, "and if you're implying for a single second that I would ever consider harming Scottie—"

"Agnes was as young and helpless as Scottie when she had the misfortune to fall foul of you."

"Father, there was a war on. And other people did far worse things to her afterwards."

Gabriel curled his hands around the teacup as though to warm them. "Perhaps it would be better if you told me exactly what happened rather than allow me to torture you in this way."

George stood up sharply and walked back to the sink, for the specific purpose, Gabriel suspected, of turning his back on his accuser. Another detail of his training perhaps. "You've heard of the Home Guard, I suspect?" asked George without turning around.

"Of course. I should have joined myself if I were allowed to bear arms these days."

"Well, Father, as you will well remember, there was a significant period during the war when Britain faced the threat of invasion. The majority of fit and able young men had been called up, and many were serving abroad. But contrary to popular belief, Mr Churchill did not leave these hallowed isles to be defended by a bunch of grandads armed with carving knives tied to broomsticks. The Home Guard were—at their best—quite well organised and well armed, but there was another, smaller, more efficient army being trained out of sight at the same time. The aim was to repel an invading force if the Germans turned up on our doorstep, but also to serve as resistance fighters if Britain were to fall. I had served in both the army and intelligence before the war started, and I had expected that I would be sent behind enemy lines, thanks to my proficiency in certain languages. But that was not to be."

Gabriel had been reluctant to interrupt, but George's narrative faltered a little at the crossroads between the acceptable and the unthinkable, and Gabriel put his teacup down. "There is nothing ignoble about defending one's country, even covertly. An agent must go where he is sent, rather like a priest." He paused, then decided to just come out with it. "Whose ridiculous idea was it to build the bunker there?"

George turned around and gave Gabriel a half smile. "I had nothing to do with the planning and building of the bunker, and there are several of them hidden around the country. Now that the war is over, they are no longer needed; most have been abandoned and will simply fall into disrepair. My understanding is that the location of that bunker was quite carefully considered. There was some sort of chamber there from long ago, an abandoned mine or something, which removed the need for expensive, noisy excavations. Besides that, the lie of the land was perfect, the area isolated without being too far from human habitation either."

"It was overlooked by a cottage," Gabriel protested. "Any Tom, Dick or Harry could have seen people coming and going."

"That's not quite true actually. There were a few more trees during the war than there are now—some blight or other a couple of years ago killed off a lot of them—so the entrance to the bunker was very easy to conceal from view of the house. The cottage could have been requisitioned— heaven knows, plenty of homes were, without compunction —but if it had been, rumours would have spread. It would have been too obvious that there were plans for the area.

The cottage acted as quite a convenient distraction in that sense. No one would ever have suspected that there was a military operation going on a few feet below ground, just yards away from a family home."

"Did your people spread the rumour about the area being haunted?"

George chuckled. "Oh no, that's a very old story. Places like this tend to be quite superstitious. Let's just say we fostered it. We made absolutely sure that no one other than that family would ever come anywhere near that stretch of ground. It was widely known that the Jenningses were reclusive types who never entertained. The father was away and then died, leaving just one woman and two children. Even the postman didn't call. It was too much of an inconvenience to get down there, or Mrs Jennings had had a falling out with him years before. She always collected her letters at the post office. Apart from the milkman, who was notoriously as blind as a bat and the *very* occasional visit from a friend, there was no one else to worry about. In any case, those bunkers were very carefully designed to be invisible even in plain sight. No one would have found it even if he were looking for it, and of course no one was."

"How did Agnes find it?"

George sighed and made his way back to his chair. "It's amazing how one tiny oversight can cause so much trouble. I think one of us dropped a cigarette end on our way down once. We didn't even use that entrance very much. She must have been playing nearby and found it. It's hard to imagine it to look at her, but as a child she was incredibly daring, and she's a great deal sharper than she lets on. Agnes must have put two and two together immediately, realised someone had been in the area who should not have been and thought it would be a jolly funny idea to go and find him. I don't know how she stumbled upon the entrance, but children do what adults virtually never do: they grub about in the grass; they get on their hands and knees and poke around. For an inquisitive child, finding a concealed entrance must have felt like falling into a storybook. Of course she couldn't help herself. She came creeping in as bold as brass, without even going back for a torch—imagine having the nerve to do that as a child? Stepping into an almost completely dark tunnel just to see what was in there."

"And you were waiting for her."

"Father, I swear I never hurt her."

"She was bruised. There were bruises on her arms."

George flinched. "If there were, they were accidental. I may have squeezed her a bit too hard as I dragged her into the main chamber. I had to get her away from the entrance as quickly as possible in case she screamed and someone else heard. One lapse in security was easy enough to take care of; two would have compromised everything. I never hurt her, but I said I would if she told anyone."

"You must have been pretty persuasive. She wouldn't tell her own mother, even when she tried to beat it out of her."

George shrugged, but all the energy had drained from him, and he talked as though he were half asleep. "I may as well come completely clean about it. She was already very badly frightened by the time I got her into the main chamber. Well, you can imagine, can't you? Someone suddenly grabbing her like that, slamming a hand over her mouth, dragging her, kicking and struggling, away from daylight. When a person is frightened, a child even more so, they are very easy to manipulate. I—well, oh, this sounds so much worse than it really was!"

"What did you do?"

"I fired a gun in her direction."

Gabriel could not hide his disgust. "You shot at a child?"

"It's all right, Father," answered George, as though the priest had misunderstood him. "I'm a dead shot. I would never have hit her accidentally, but she wasn't to know that. The gun was fitted with a silencer, but even if it hadn't been, I doubt anyone would have heard the shot anyway."

"She was missing for hours. There was more to it than that, wasn't there?"

George refused to look up. "I may have had to reinforce the message several times before we could risk letting her go. And in any case, we knew people would be looking for her and we couldn't just release her into broad daylight like that, or she might have been seen. It was the only time that patch of ground might be searched. So we kept her in the bunker, repeating the message to her over and over again that she saw nothing, that she could not remember a thing. We couldn't even risk giving her a cover story because lies can be unravelled quite quickly, and if there were any holes in her story, it would have become obvious that she was hiding something. Then it might not be long before someone began to join the dots."

"So you simply repeated to her that she had seen nothing and threatened her with death if she told anyone what she *had* seen, knowing that silence was safer for you than a plausible story?"

George gave him a look that Gabriel did not care for very

much. "You know, you're quite good at this. You would have done pretty well in intelligence."

"I'd rather do my fighting out in the open, if it's all the same to you," remarked Gabriel.

"Someone's got to do it."

"I wish I had a shilling for every time someone has said that to me," answered Gabriel, feeling an unusual stirring of temper. "I have already said that there is nothing wrong with serving one's country, but there are laws even in wartime. How close to Agnes' head did that bullet get?"

George was on his feet, and Gabriel suspected he would have raised his voice if it were not for the risk of being overheard. "I would never have killed her, Father. Yes, I fired very close indeed, inches away from her head, and I will never forget the sound of her screaming. I had to force a rag into her mouth just to stop the noise, not because I thought anyone would hear but because I couldn't bear the sound of it. But I needed her to believe that I really would shoot her dead if she told a soul what she had seen. And if you think me so very brutal, please consider, Father, that if there had been an invasion, I might have had to kill her."

Gabriel jumped off his stool, almost unsettling the cups and saucers as he did so. "Are you seriously telling me you would have considered shooting a child? Precisely how dirty was the dirty war?"

The two men stood only inches apart like duellers awaiting the signal to draw. George glanced momentarily towards the door before responding. "Father, if there had been an occupation and word had got out that little Agnes Jennings was in possession of information that the Gestapo would be very, very interested to hear, her life would not have been worth living. And many other lives might well have been at risk."

Gabriel looked George steadily in the eye. "And could you have done it? Could you really have lured a child to her death like that, for any reason?"

George was the first to break eye contact. "It would have been quick and painless. A bullet to the back of the head is not such a terrible way to go. And the Allies killed a good many children in much crueller ways, in Berlin, in Tokyo, in Hiroshima . . ."

"That is not what I asked you."

George made a sound that might almost have been a whimper coming from anyone else, and Gabriel realised, to his astonishment, that the man was in tears. "I don't know. I don't know if it would even have come to that. Perhaps, perhaps I could have been convinced that she really had forgotten that she'd seen the place. Perhaps I could have found some way of spiriting her away to somewhere safe until it was all over. I'm simply grateful that I was never forced to make a decision. But then I think there are a great many of us who were relieved the occupation never came, not just because of what it would have meant for the country but because of the choices we would have had to make."

George collapsed into the rocking chair, causing it to creak backwards a little too violently and knock against the edge of one of the bookshelves. The collision made a crack so loud, he instinctively threw his head into his hands, bracing for an explosion. Gabriel stepped towards him and put a hand on his shoulder. "Thank you," said Gabriel. "I know it was very hard for you to tell me all that, and I will not share it unless I absolutely have to. You are not responsible for what Enid Jennings did to Agnes that day, but I think you have always known the terrible harm her encounter with you had on her life."

"If I could have stopped her finding out, if I could go back in time and pick up that bloody cigarette end . . ." Gabriel did not need to hear any more. The room felt suddenly oppressive. Gabriel was aware of the distant murmur of people coming and going on the pavement outside the shop and the frittering away of valuable minutes.

"Mr Smithson," said Gabriel finally, "I am sorry to ask this of you, but Agnes' life may well be in danger again. If you let her hang for a crime she did not commit or be imprisoned in an asylum for the rest of her life because the authorities believe her to be mad, you will be accountable for her life as surely as if you had shot her that day. I need to ask you a few more questions. Nothing to do with you or your life or even your guilt, but I do need your help."

George refused to move for several minutes, but Gabriel's patience had the effect of unnerving him, and he eventually sat up. "You're not going to go away, are you?"

"No, I'm not. It's all right; this is the easy bit. I need to know about this bunker. Could Enid Jennings also have known about it?"

"No. If Agnes did not tell her, then I can't see how she could have known."

"Are you sure?"

George looked up at Gabriel in exasperation. "Father, Mrs Jennings was a nasty, cantankerous old schoolmistress. That is all she was. If you think she was killed because she was up to her scrawny old neck in some conspiracy, please put it out of your mind. Whoever killed her probably did so for quite trivial reasons. Hate can get out of control quite quickly in a person, I have discovered, and she was hated by many, many people in this town."

"Do the police know about the bunker?" George shook his head. "Then why didn't you tell them about it? It would have saved a great deal of confusion if you had."

"It's not my job to tell the Bobbies how to do theirs," George answered contemptuously. "It's been almost amusing watching them scratching their wooden heads, trying to puzzle it all out."

Gabriel felt his temper stirring again. "Mr Smithson, if you had told the police how Enid Jennings came to disappear under her daughter's nose, you might have saved Agnes a great deal of suffering. She would not have had her sanity called into question, and she is unlikely to have been labelled a suspect."

George stood up, with what was almost sulkiness. "What do you want?"

"I want you to take me down there. Now, before Douglas Jennings goes home."

11

It was already dark by the time the two men had descended the hill, and even the powerful beam of George's torch gave Gabriel little reassurance. "Imagine coming this way every evening throughout the winter," he whispered to George. "One would lose the will to live."

"Not afraid of ghosts, are you, Father?" George teased, and Gabriel had a nasty sense that the other man was quite enjoying watching him sweat. On the move, in the company of a man who was less sure of himself than he was, George was in his element, the spectres of the past hour temporarily banished.

"No, I'm not afraid of ghosts," Gabriel snapped, betraying his nerves. "I am, however, distinctly nervous of the living, particularly at a murder scene. If we could just get on with it . . ."

"I doubt what you are about to see was the murder scene," George answered, and Gabriel noticed him concentrating on the ground below him as they edged their way along the path. Gabriel was aware of the old dead tree and the paving stones of the path he had rather foolishly hoped to lift up earlier in the investigation. George got down on his knees, handing Gabriel the torch. "Shine the beam directly on this patch of grass," he instructed, and Gabriel watched in astonishment as George ran his fingers along the edge of the path and rolled back a section of grass that looked as lush and natural as all the rest. In the pale circle of light, Gabriel could see what would have passed as natural stone to an onlooker if, by some mishap, the grass covering had moved or been allowed to wear away.

"Well I'm dashed!" was all he could say, as George very carefully began to prise open the trap door. "It's indistinguishable from the outside!"

"We're quite clever chaps when we have to be," George answered, pulling open the door to reveal a vast, empty black space beneath them. "People think of pulling up paving stones, but no one ever imagines that humble grass might be covering anything. Would you like me to lead the way?"

"I'd be delighted," muttered Gabriel, shrinking from the prospect of the earth swallowing him like that. "How on earth did you get in and out without anybody noticing?"

"As a matter of fact, Father," George answered, seating himself at the edge of the hole so that he could feel the steps under his feet before he began scrambling down, taking the torch with him. "Are you coming?" Gabriel braced himself and followed, hoping against all hope that his hypothesis about George Smithson was correct. "As a matter of fact, we rarely used this entrance. In spite of all our precautions, we generally preferred the other way in. We tended to come in and out this way only between certain hours when we had the added cover of darkness."

Gabriel was aware that he was being led down a short, extremely steep set of stairs before he found himself on the flat again. George waited until he had settled before brushing past him, ascending the stairs again very quickly and closing off the entrance. Gabriel felt a terrifying sense that he was being buried alive as the door closed with a thud; he wondered what must have gone through little Agnes' mind when she found herself in the hands of hostile strangers, being dragged deeper and deeper into this vast grave. He whispered a quiet Paternoster to himself to steady his nerves.

"Put these on," said George, pressing a pair of leather gloves into Gabriel's hands. "It's best not to leave any fingerprints. Now, if you'll follow me, I'll show you what I think you need to see. How fit are you?"

"Fit enough, I hope." Gabriel felt unnerved again, this time by the damp acoustic which seemed to stifle everything they said as soon as it was out of their mouths. "Why do you ask?"

"Because it's a good mile to the other end of the bunker."

"One mile!"

"Yes, it comes out at the river. Waterways were very useful for . . ." He trailed off, aware of Gabriel glaring daggers at him through the darkness. "Yes, I know. There was never any mystery about how Enid Jennings' body came to be washed up at Port Shaston, having disappeared here. Someone who knew about the bunker lured her and dragged her down here against her will. The question is whether she died immediately and her body was carried all the way to the river or she was forced to walk there and was killed at the other end."

"It rather mitigates against my hope that she was not murdered at all."

"I thought that much was obvious."

Gabriel rounded on George, determined not to be distracted. "Mr Smithson, I hope you feel the smallest modicum of shame about what you have done. You knew Agnes' story made perfect sense. *All of it.* You knew she had nothing to do with this. You could have spared her so much misery!"

"Look here, if I had told the police everything, I would have fallen under suspicion myself," George explained matter-of-factly. "Who else knows about the existence of this place? Who else could have killed her? Frankly, Father, you're taking a hell of a risk coming down here with me when you know I am the most likely person to have killed her in such a way."

"I know you may have done it," Gabriel said, "but I suspect that you have been trained to commit murder and make it look like an accident. If you wanted to kill me, you would find a way to do it wherever I was, even perhaps in the abbey. So, it makes very little odds that I choose to come to a deserted place like this with you."

"You're a brave man," was all George could find to say, handing Gabriel back the torch as though to indicate that he meant him no harm. "I'm not sure I trust the battery on that torch to last out as long as we need, and we need more light anyway to make a proper search. Wait a moment while I get the lights on."

Gabriel stood stock-still, pointing the torch in George's direction as the man removed a panel in the wall and, after some creaking and fumbling, threw a switch that flooded the tunnel with light. "I didn't realise there was electricity down here," commented Gabriel, his eyes screwed tightly shut. The light from the overhead bulbs was hardly dazzling, but after the near darkness of the past few minutes, it startled him with its intensity.

"This bunker was quite well equipped once," answered George, taking the torch from Gabriel's shaking hands, "though I am a little surprised the wiring still works. We had better not stay down here too long. By the time we have walked to the other side and back, Douglas may well be home, and I'd rather not meet him, if it's all the same to you."

"I thought this place was well concealed?"

"It is! How many times do I have to tell you? It may not have occurred to you, however, that if Douglas sees the two of us walking around in the vicinity at this hour, he will expect an explanation, and I'd rather not have to deal with all of that."

Gabriel shrugged with the resignation of a man who knows perfectly well he is not being told the truth and got down to the business of looking around him. "Smithson, I want you to tell me if you see anything amiss, any sign that the bunker has been used for anything other than its intended purpose. I dare say you were the last person to live down here."

George nodded and set to work, leaving Gabriel looking around indecisively. Everything about the bunker felt chillingly hostile, not just the fact that it had been built underground in time of war but the whole uninhabited feel of the place. It had been built as a refuge in time of national crisis, meant to hide a group of hardy young patriots prepared to risk torture and death in defence of their country. Every detail of the main chamber looked like a monument to the darkest moments of a nation's darkest hour. The chamber was high enough for a man as tall as George Smithson to stand up comfortably with some six inches above his head; there was a table and several chairs stacked to one side but little else in the way of furnishings. What looked like several oblong boxes rested at either end, and Gabriel instinctively moved towards them.

"You won't find anything in there," said George, reading Gabriel's mind. "They're not for storage. If we had to sleep down here, they could be used as makeshift beds. It's not very healthy to lie flat on the floor when one is this far down. Aha!"

Gabriel looked in the direction George was pointing, where something small and metallic glistened in a corner. Gabriel stepped forward and bent down, picking up a good-quality penknife, the main blade partially opened. "Douglas will be pleased," he said dryly, but the more he looked at the blade, the more innocuous it looked.

"Why? Was he hoping to hide the murder weapon?"

"I knew when I came down here that Enid Jennings was not stabbed," said Gabriel, kneeling back down on the floor, which until recently had been covered in an undisturbed film of dust. He was distracted for a moment by movement he saw out of the corner of his eye and almost fell over backwards at the sight of a large spider spinning in a corner. He swallowed his queasiness and looked back at the floor. "How many pairs of footprints do you suppose?"

George glanced at the mess of footprints on top of footprints on top of more footprints. When the two men turned to look behind them, the many sets of prints petered out and were replaced by a bizarre-looking path that stretched away into the darkness beyond their sight, as though someone had attempted to clean the floor and done a very slapdash job of it. "Besides us, I'd say that only two people came down here, one of them unwillingly, and that perhaps someone has attempted to cover their tracks. Do you really want to walk all the way along, Father? I'll not try to stop you, but it might be easier to come back tomorrow, early, while there are a good few hours of daylight left."

Gabriel ignored George and turned to look at the wall opposite the table. In spite of the grime and the cobwebs that had accumulated, Gabriel could just make out a small chink in the stone. "Is that where you shot at Agnes?" he asked tonelessly.

George bristled in the dour light. "If you have quite finished playing Sherlock Holmes, Father, I would quite like to get out of here."

Gabriel nodded. "Let's. I'm fairly sure that any evidence at the other end would have been washed away by now, and in any case, I have seen everything I needed to see. The real drama happened here, not at the river."

"I do wish you wouldn't talk in riddles," George complained, switching the torch back on. "Here, take the torch. I'll turn out the lights now, if you don't mind. Time to go." He stepped back in the direction of the panel, unconsciously avoiding stepping on the footprints as though afraid of contaminating the evidence.

"There is something else that puzzles me."

"Oh yes? And what might that be?"

"How has Agnes never recognised you?"

George turned back to face him in the weak light. "She never saw my face, Father. Our faces were partially covered, and we turned out the main lights so that she could never get a good look at us. And I'm very good at disguising my voice. It comes from speaking other languages. I needed to be sure I could never be identified."

"That whole ordeal took place in virtual darkness? Poor little thing; it gets worse and worse."

"I think you have made your point."

Gabriel hesitated. "There was one other thing. Did you retire from your profession or were you thrown out for overstepping the mark too many times? I don't believe you were ordered to threaten that poor—"

George turned on him, his temper finally snapping. "Why can't you mind your own bloody business? My change of profession has nothing to do with anything!"

A split second later, the men were startled by the sound of footsteps near them and froze.

"Were we followed?" mouthed Gabriel, not daring to look behind him.

George put a finger to his lips and, with a razor-sharp reflexive movement, grabbed Gabriel's arm and threw him in the direction of the table. "Take cover!" he hissed, as he grabbed the torch—switching it off—and held it out in front of him. Gabriel crouched behind the table, grateful for its heaviness, then looked up in time to see a figure flying at George. The assailant was powerfully built and in a terrible rage, but George had the advantage and slammed the torch against the side of the man's head, knocking him down. Gabriel stood up and saw Douglas Jennings struggling to his feet, white-faced and trembling with anger. Signs of blood appeared across his temple. He swung an expert punch at George's face, but George took hold of his wrist and twisted his arm into a half nelson, forcing him onto his knees. "What the devil do you think you're playing at?" snarled George, and there was something infinitely more frightening about George Smithson's quiet rage than a raised voice would have been. "I could have broken your neck!"

It would not take much, thought Gabriel as he stepped slowly towards the two men, Douglas still struggling to free himself in spite of the helplessness of his position. *It would not take much to turn either of you into killers.* He said, "It's all right, Smithson. Let him stand up. I don't think he means either of us any harm."

George loosened his grip on Douglas with the utmost reluctance, but stood over him in such a threatening way that Douglas hesitated before attempting to stand, as though half expecting to be knocked down again. "I knew there had to be something here," said Douglas, looking accusingly at George. "When Agnes got herself into a state just off the path, I knew she must be remembering something. Even she didn't realise what was happening, but I knew. It's happened to me since the war, that sudden feeling as though one is back there again, exactly where the worst thing happened."

"A flashback?" ventured Gabriel.

Douglas did not look in Gabriel's direction. "I couldn't find anything, but I came home from work early today and saw the two of you walking this way."

"In that case, you should have made yourself known to us," said Gabriel, but Douglas was not even looking at him.

"It was your baby, wasn't it?" he demanded, grabbing at George's lapels and to Gabriel's surprise, George made no attempt at throwing him off. "You used to bring her down here, didn't you? I knew something terrible had happened to her that day, but she wouldn't talk to me, and by the time our mother had finished on her, she wouldn't talk to anyone. Then, before I knew it, I was in uniform, halfway to Italy."

George pushed Douglas away with unexpected gentleness. "I've no idea what you're talking about, Jennings," he said, and Gabriel knew he meant it. "What baby?"

Douglas attempted to fly at George again, but George got hold of both his wrists this time and forced him back against the wall. "You pervert! I know what you did to her!" shouted Douglas, struggling like a man possessed. "No one was supposed to know! I wasn't supposed to know, but she woke up screaming in the night: 'My baby! My baby!' You brought her down here, didn't you? It's perfect; no one would ever have known what you were doing!"

"Don't be a bloody fool, Jennings! I don't know what you're talking about!"

Gabriel stepped between them, gesturing at George to let go of Douglas. "Gentlemen, perhaps we should take this argument somewhere else. You are standing exactly in the place a woman died."

~

If anything, the Jennings' cottage felt even less welcoming than on the first occasion Gabriel had entered. In Agnes' absence, the house had become untidy. The drawing room, into which Douglas marched them unceremoniously, was littered with piles of papers and books, and Gabriel noticed empty and half-empty glasses cluttering up the various surfaces. "Please forgive the state of the place," said Douglas unapologetically. "I'm in the process of sorting out my mother's things. Not a pleasant task under the circumstances."

"I quite understand," said Gabriel, hesitating before finding himself a seat. "How did your mother leave her affairs?"

"That's absolutely none of your business," Douglas retorted, sitting down himself without inviting George to do so. George shrugged, then sat on the sofa next to Gabriel, as though determining him to be an ally. "My mother was an extremely particular woman, and I doubted she would have left her affairs in anything other than perfect order. Which, of course, she did. Does that answer your question?"

"Thank you," said Gabriel. He noted that Douglas was making a point of not offering any refreshment to either of them, but his anger was directed entirely at George. Gabriel endeavoured to create a distraction and held out the penknife. "I found this down there."

Douglas looked at him in surprise before snatching the knife out of his hands. "I had assumed it was at the bottom of the river. What is the meaning of all this?"

"It means," Gabriel explained, "that your sister was telling the truth and was in her right mind all along. Someone lay in wait and pulled your mother into that bunker at the precise second Agnes was attending to the kettle. It would not have taken long at all for her to disappear, and it may have been completely coincidental that she vanished at exactly the moment Agnes was not looking. In fact, my suspicion is that whoever did it had not expected there to be anyone at home."

"Then who did it?" demanded Douglas, placing the penknife in his lap, unable to bring himself to put it away. "Tell me which man is responsible for this!"

"I didn't say it was a man," Gabriel corrected him, "and as yet, I'm afraid I cannot answer your question. However, I am coming to the belief that your mother may have died shortly before she could be murdered."

Douglas looked at Gabriel as though the man were speaking gibberish. "What are you talking about? Was my mother murdered, or wasn't she?"

Gabriel hesitated. In his uncertainty, he knew he was taking another gamble, but he also knew that if he were right, the results of the postmortem would reveal the truth before long anyway. "I'm beginning to suspect that whoever dragged your mother into the chamber had every intention of killing her. There were signs of a struggle down there, and your mother had time to reach for the penknife and begin to open it, almost certainly to defend herself. However, there were no bloodstains on the ground or on that knife, so I doubt if she got beyond the process of opening the thing."

Douglas stood up abruptly and made for the door. "I don't have to listen to any of this nonsense. I'm calling the police."

"I suggest you do that," said Gabriel, ignoring George's obvious agitation beside him. "If nothing else, the revelations of this evening should help your sister's case."

"Father, please!" George began. "We need to find out who else knew about the bunker. If we can't come out with any plausible names, the police will arrest me in a trice."

Douglas glanced back at George with a look of contempt on his face that reminded Gabriel horribly of the way his dead mother had looked at Pamela. "I have every intention of ensuring they do, Smithson. I know it was you. You're the one who forced yourself on my sister; you're the only one who knew about that bunker. Did my mother find out that you were the father and confront you?"

"No—"

"It's just the sort of thing she would have done. It wouldn't occur to her she might get hurt. How did she find out it was you?"

George rose to his feet with an air of weary frustration. "For pity's sake, Jennings, I had nothing to do with any baby. I had no idea Agnes had had a baby until you were indiscreet enough to say so."

"I think there may have been a misunderstanding here, gentlemen," Gabriel put in, standing between the two men yet again, though there was a good deal more space between them now. "What do you mean by a baby?"

"Why not ask him, Father?" demanded Douglas, jabbing a finger in George's chest. George did not move. "Why not ask him to confess?"

"Jennings, I did nothing of the sort to your sister," said George quietly, but he looked as shocked as Gabriel. "You must believe me. I never touched her. I had no idea there was a child."

"There isn't," answered Douglas coldly. "The baby died, born too early. I was away at the time. I had no idea she had ever been pregnant until I overheard that nightmare. Mother said that Agnes had nearly died, and if she ever found out who had done such a terrible thing to her daughter, she would expose him. She would make him pay, whoever he was."

George sank back into the sofa. "I'm so sorry, old man, but I truly had no idea. I did have an encounter with Agnes, but only when she was a child, and I swear on my life I never violated her. Even if you imagine me capable of such a crime, do you think it likely I would have chanced it when I could not risk being noticed by anyone?"

Douglas did not soften in the least, but Gabriel could see the beginnings of doubt creeping over him. "There's a certain sort of man who thinks he can take what he pleases," answered Douglas. "I came across a few of those among our own. I don't know what you're capable of, Smithson, but I don't believe in anyone's innocence anymore."

Gabriel indicated for George to sit down again and turned to Douglas. "I think you should call the constabulary and let Applegate know that we have discovered the place where your mother died and how her body came to be washed up at Port Shaston. But it seems to be quite clear now that there is a great deal more to this than we realised. I cannot vouch for Mr Smithson here, but I think it would be unwise to jump to any conclusions."

"What about this baby?" asked George, tersely. "Do we inform Applegate? I dare say he would prefer to know."

Gabriel noticed Douglas flushing red at the accusatory reference. As a lawyer used to dealing with delicate, confidential situations, he had realised his terrible lapse in judgement if Smithson truly knew nothing about Agnes' baby. "If it's all the same to you, Mr Smithson," Gabriel suggested, "I think we should refrain from mentioning anything about this story, since none of us can prove it happened. If Agnes has never spoken of it, we have no right to spread gossip."

"It is hardly spreading gossip to furnish the police with

the facts," George objected, "especially if we are to assume that it was a factor in Enid Jennings' murder."

"The words 'pot', 'kettle' and 'black' spring to mind," answered Gabriel, more angrily than he had intended, but he was beginning to wonder what George was playing at. "The considerably more important information you with-held was damaging only to yourself. I insist that we do not speak of this unless Agnes herself chooses to do so. If she did indeed lose a baby, she has the right to keep this to herself if she so chooses."

"I agree," said Douglas, a little too readily. "I should never have broached the subject in the first place. I was just so sure Smithson here was involved." Douglas got up to make the phone call, but lingered in the doorway again. "Before I ring the constabulary, Father, perhaps you could tell us what you discovered today? You seem very sure that my mother died in that spot. May I ask why?"

Gabriel was aware of the two men scrutinising his every move and faltered under the weight of his own common sense. He did not know who was responsible, and therefore everyone to whom he spoke might be the guilty party, in-cluding these two men who had both been trained to kill and might both have had the means or motive to do so. Gabriel mentally held his most precious cards to his chest and cleared his throat: "Well, it is quite obvious to me that she died in that chamber, thanks to all those footprints, which suggests a struggle. Frankly, it is hard to imagine any self-respecting person going down into such a place willingly. The presence of the penknife painted the picture of a person who knew she was in mortal danger and was attempting to defend her-self but never had the chance."

"It would have been a clumsy weapon even in expert hands," Douglas commented, "even if she had had the time to draw the thing."

"Indeed, but in a moment of desperation it may have been all she could have thought of," Gabriel responded. "The other detail I noticed, of course, was the odd pattern of dust further down. The way it appeared to have been swept up clearly demonstrated to me that she died in situ and her body was dragged the length of the tunnel. She had a graze on her heel, which could have been caused by her being dragged along the riverbed or along a stone surface. I suspect that a search along the tunnel might reveal the missing shoe. Her long coat and skirt would have had the effect of brushing the path clean of dust, and any dust that accumulated on her clothing would have washed away in the river."

"I see," answered Douglas, looking down into the corner of the room. Gabriel wondered what the man could be feeling. It had been impossible from the start for him to pretend he had felt any great affection for his mother, but in the end, he was still the son of a dead woman being told the exact location of her death, being told that she had almost certainly died frightened and fully aware that she was about to meet a violent end. "But who could have done such a thing? I mean, who would go to such bizarre lengths to kill a woman? There are so many easier ways it could have been done."

"I think it goes without saying that we are looking at an extremely intelligent person," commented Gabriel, hoping to look as transparent as possible when he was going out of his way to reveal as little of importance as he could. "A patient person."

"Patient?"

"You know the old saying: beware the wrath of a patient man—or woman? It seems very clear to me that whoever carried out this act planned it very carefully indeed. Whoever did it wanted to make absolutely certain that he would never be found out. There are indeed many other ways to murder a woman, but in a small town there are not quite as many hiding places as one would imagine. The trouble is that the best-laid plans have a tendency to go awry when they involve third parties who are unaware of their part. Enid Jennings was not supposed to die where she did. Who would drag a dead body such a distance when it would be just as easy to force her to walk that way and then kill her at the other end? And why risk there being a witness unless the person concerned knew that Agnes could be discredited or implicated?"

George got up abruptly, signalling to Gabriel to do the same. "Look here, Father, I think we have imposed quite long enough on this gentleman's time. He needs to speak to the inspector, and we both need to get home. I'm sure Fr Foley will be wondering where on earth you are."

Gabriel had a sinking feeling Fr Foley would certainly want to know where he had been since before lunch, and he did not fancy much having to make his explanations. He could not help wanting to leave Douglas Jennings' sullen company for the safety of the presbytery, but he was curious as to why George was so keen to break up the meeting. He played along. "You are quite right, Mr Smithson. It is getting late, and I promised Father I would be home in good time to dinner." He nodded in Douglas' direction. "Please pass on my best wishes to your sister," he said. "If you would like me to go and see her again—"

"I really don't think that will be necessary, Father," answered Douglas quickly. "If Applegate can be persuaded to leave her alone, I will get her out of that place directly. In the morning, if possible."

Thank the Lord for small mercies then, thought Gabriel, as he walked in silence next to George Smithson up the hill. *If I can do no more than persuade the inspector that Agnes is innocent of any blame, it will be enough.* "Thank you for your assistance," he said to George when they reached a parting of ways without having exchanged a single word in the darkness. George simply nodded in acknowledgement and walked away in the opposite direction without offering his companion a word of explanation.

There were one or two other details Gabriel had not seen fit to share with the two men, but which he suspected might prove more damning than any other piece of evidence. Whoever had pulled Enid Jennings down into that cavern had gone to some lengths to avoid hurting her. It was no mean feat to drag a grown woman down a steep flight of stairs without causing her any harm, and her body had shown no sign of a violent struggle. It was virtually beyond doubt, as far as Gabriel was concerned, that the person responsible had planned murder and yet had somehow hesitated when it came to it, long enough for Enid Jennings to reach into her handbag and pull out the penknife. A gentle murderer? Gabriel walked along the quiet streets, wishing good evening to the few people he passed, but he could not fight off the overwhelming sense of fear that was overtaking him. *O God, send me home*, he prayed, *please send me home*. Gabriel had felt lonely many times before, but it was a long time since he had felt quite so afraid.

12

"Holy Mother, you look as though you've been body snatching!" exclaimed an incredulous voice when Gabriel tiptoed into the house, praying that Fr Foley might be out. Fr Foley was very much in, staring across the room at him as he removed his filthy coat. "Where in heaven's name have you been all day? You're supposed to be assisting a poorly old man. I had to take your catechism class."

Gabriel threw his head into his hands. "Father, I am so sorry. I'm so sorry, I clean forgot. I had to return to the abbey urgently. I should have sent a message to you. One thing led to another . . ."

Fr Foley shook his head, sending off waves of invisible reproach. It was the first time Gabriel had had the sense that he was trying the old man's patience. "I cannot imagine that you went to the abbey on an errand of mercy. Now what have you been up to?"

Gabriel looked at his coat as he hung it carefully on the coat stand; even the dim light of the hall failed to disguise how dirty it was, covered with dust and cobwebs. To complement the effect, his shoes were encrusted with mud, but almost more incriminating were the leather gloves he had neglected to return to George Smithson, which completed the image of a burglar on his way back from a job. All he needed was a large sack labelled *swag*. "I'm afraid I've had rather a frightful afternoon," said Gabriel quietly, playing for sympathy, which he doubted he deserved. "I discovered the place where Enid Jennings died—"

"I thought she had died in the river," Fr Foley interrupted. "You don't look as though you've been fishing."

"She didn't die anywhere near the river," said Gabriel. "It was horrible, like discovering that a person has been buried alive. I know she was a disagreeable woman, but I can't bear the thought of her dying frightened and trapped like that. I'm afraid I don't think I shall sleep very well tonight."

Fr Foley's look of disapproval softened almost immediately, and he gestured to the kitchen table, where their dinners had evidently just been laid out. Gabriel saw the steam floating off plates and smelt hot pastry wafting in his direction. "Is that really a Cornish pasty?" asked Gabriel, salivating at the sight of that bulging semicircle of golden pastry on the plate, promising minced beef and onions and other delights, except that he knew perfectly well it would contain no such luxuries.

"Apparently," answered Fr Foley, "just don't spoil the evening by asking what's actually in them. The mashed potato is real enough, though." Gabriel sat down gratefully and bowed his head as Fr Foley said grace before sitting down opposite him. "It seems to me that you haven't been sleeping well for a few nights now, son. Would you like me to give you one of my sedatives?"

"Is that allowed?" asked Gabriel, but a moment later he was in ersatz Cornish pasty–flavoured heaven and could not have cared if Fr Foley had laced his tea with laudanum. There was clearly no beef or onions in the pasty, but he could taste lightly salted vegetables and a delicate splash of gravy to complement the soft bits of potato.

"They're perfectly safe if they're being given to a man with a dicky ticker like mine," promised Fr Foley, tucking into his own dinner with a little less enthusiasm. "Where did she die?"

"Just yards away from her own home. The whole thing is the stuff of nightmares. First time I have felt afraid since . . ." He stared at his plate, thrown by an unfamiliar sensation prickling his eyes. He endeavoured to stop himself from blinking until the moist, heavy feeling had left his eyelids. He was aware of Fr Foley watching him solicitously and of the need to break the silence before it became any more suspicious. "Father, if you don't mind my asking, when did you enter seminary?"

Fr Foley blinked in surprise. "I entered the aspirantate at eleven, junior seminary when I was thirteen. Why?"

"Have you ever looked back?"

The old man considered for a moment before saying casually, "Never," and filling his mouth with food as though to draw attention to the silliness of the question. When Gabriel failed to make any response, he swallowed and said, "Not having any wee doubts now, are we?"

Gabriel shook his head, too dejected to be offended. "Not at all."

Fr Foley sighed. "I'd forgotten, the best wine was left until last with you, wasn't it?"

"I'm not sure about that," said Gabriel softly, "but yes, I did arrive a little late in the day. But by the time I entered seminary, there wasn't very much to look back to."

175

Fr Foley got up and filled Gabriel's glass for him, patting him on the shoulder as he did so. "You're run down, my boy, that's all. Get outside of that food and let me get you something to make you sleep. A good night's rest—that's all you need."

Fr Foley obviously had a point, because Gabriel woke up next morning with the serene feeling of a man who has enjoyed eight hours of drugged, dreamless sleep. The effects of the sedatives—which, contrary to Fr Foley's promise, had proven to be quite powerful—were to leave Gabriel feeling drowsy and somewhat detached from the rest of the world as he got himself up, wandered over to the church and said Mass. It was rather like looking at the world through a thin glass tube. Everything was as it should be, and he was as he should be but just a little separated from it all.

He knew he had a busy afternoon and could not afford to let Fr Foley down again, so he made his way directly to Pamela Milton's family home without stopping to break his fast, an omission that made him feel only more light-headed and separate from everything around him. He wondered whether it would make him more objective, this sense of being outside of things, but by the time he reached the smart neighbourhood of Queen Victoria Road, with its grand redbrick houses surrounded by trees and expansive lawns, Gabriel could feel himself falling back down to earth with a bump.

The Miltons were well-to-do and unashamedly so, the recipients of family money or good fortune in business. Gabriel found, when he reached the family residence, that he had to ring the bell at the front gates to gain entrance, a practice almost unheard of in this trusting little town. Moments later, he looked through the slats of the wooden gates —put there to replace metal railings, he suspected—and saw Scottie bounding towards him like a boisterous Labrador, her face pink with the cold morning air.

"Good morning!" She greeted him warmly, lifting the latch and heaving the gate open. "Come in."

"That was quick!" answered Gabriel, gratefully, following her into the garden. He spotted a treehouse in the near corner and realised that Scottie must have been playing outside and seen him coming; hence her rapid appearance.

"I was watching the road for spies," Scottie explained, curling her hands around her eyes to suggest binoculars. "Then I saw you. Oh well, I suppose you *could* be a spy." She reached out and took his hand without a second thought, walking with him in the direction of the front door. "I suppose you've come to see my mother?"

"Yes, I have."

Scottie had the easy confidence and trust of a child growing up surrounded by adult company, which had made her charmingly precocious rather than spoilt—Gabriel suspected Pamela would be far too sensible a parent to overindulge a child, even a precious only child with a war-hero father. "Uncle George calls you Sherlock Holmes, but I said that was silly. You don't have a magnifying glass or one of those hats, though I do believe Sherlock Holmes hadn't a wife either."

Gabriel found his companion disarming and could think of little else to say other than, "Well, I suppose I could buy myself a deer-stalker hat."

Scottie shook her head impatiently. "I'm not sure priests are supposed to wear things like that, are they?"

Scottie's mother had evidently heard her daughter's prattling from inside the house and threw open the front door before Gabriel could attempt the social nicety of knocking. Pamela wore a look of affectionate exasperation and immediately put her hands on her hips. "I do hope you haven't bored Father to death already?" she asked, planting herself firmly between Scottie and the comfort of the inside. "And where do you think you're going with those muddy boots, young lady?"

Scottie looked sheepishly at her gumboots, which were plastered in mud and dead leaves. "I thought it might be time for elevenses," she said hopefully.

"You've barely finished your breakfast," answered Pamela, pointing outside. "Go on. Father is here on very secret business, so you had better keep sentry duty until he's left. We don't want any nasty eavesdroppers coming in."

Scottie sighed resignedly. "You're getting me out of the way," she said matter-of-factly. "May I have my elevenses in the treehouse today then?"

The two females exchanged knowing looks. Gabriel suspected that their domestic life was full of little moments of negotiation such as this. "Very well. I'll ask Marion to bring you out some milk and biscuits later. All right?"

Scottie gave her an approving smile, turned away from the adults and ran back in the direction of the treehouse. Pamela turned to Gabriel and gestured to him to come in.

"Sorry to drop in on you like this," Gabriel began, wiping his feet thoroughly on the doormat and unbuttoning his coat, which was looking more presentable this morning after

178

some emergency cleaning work. The hall of the house had a feeling of restrained grandeur about it, with its polished wooden floors and broad staircase up one side, which made him feel a bit shabby by comparison. "Please don't force Scottie to stay out in the cold on my account."

"It's quite all right, Father," said Pamela, cheerfully, leading him into a vast, richly furnished drawing room. "I daresay you haven't come for a quick cup of tea and an appeal for the roof fund, have you?"

Gabriel found Pamela's courteously direct approach as disarming as her daughter's, but he took a seat near the roaring fire whilst Pamela stepped back into the hall to hang up his coat and hat. The room looked as though it had once been two much smaller rooms, which had been knocked through, leaving a central arch where the old wall had been. There was a clear division between the cosy end of the room, in which he was seated, and the far end, where a grand piano stood under a cloth covering and various paintings hung on the walls, separated by mirrors that gave the room an even larger feel. In the bay window, which overlooked the garden, a pleasant little reading corner had been arranged, with two low bookcases and a recently upholstered armchair in the middle, which could be separated from the rest of the room by drawing the curtains across. Gabriel's gaze was drawn to a photograph in a silver frame, in the centre of the mantelpiece. A young man in a military cap, the male version of Pamela's face, gazed very seriously at some undefined point in the distance, as though staring at his family across the lost years.

Pamela was at his side. "I've asked Marion to bring us some tea. Now," she said, settling herself into the chair op-

179

posite, "how may I help you? I was going to visit Agnes this afternoon if Mother could spare the car."

"That's very good of you," said Gabriel, "but it is my hope that Agnes will not be in there very much longer."

"I sincerely hope not," Pamela agreed, "but at least it keeps her away from the police. I got the impression from Mr Smithson that you were trying to work it out yourself?"

Another unavoidably direct question; it wasn't quite cricket somehow. "Well," he began, steeling himself. "I should like to get to the bottom of this, and you're quite right that I have come to talk to you about it."

"Naturally."

"I shan't keep you away from your book for too long, Dr Milton, but I should like to ask you a question or two, if that's all right?"

Pamela made a passable act of indifference, but he could see the muscles tightening in her face and knew she was clenching her teeth. "Not at all, Father, though I do wish you'd call me Pamela. I feel as though I'm back in a lecture hall."

"Pamela, then. Thank you."

"Well, I told the police all I can remember from that afternoon, which isn't very much really. I'm not sure there is much more I can tell you."

"It is not the afternoon I was thinking about, as a matter of fact," Gabriel began, suppressing his own unfortunate memory of the last time he had asked Pamela a personal question. "I was thinking of the threat Enid Jennings made to you on the evening of your lecture."

"Father, she was a nasty old trout who said something idiotic," answered Pamela icily. "If you are going to insinuate that I had anything to do with her death because she made a threat she could never have carried out, then please consider the matter closed. I had nothing to do with her death."

"You hated her."

"That's a non sequitur," answered Pamela immediately. "She was a vile old bat, and we despised one another. But you must know by now that *everyone* despised her. I'm not sorry she's dead, but nor do I rejoice. Her life meant nothing to me."

He came out with it. "Pamela, why were you expelled from school?"

"What has that to do with the price of fish?" she exclaimed, but her eyes flashed with anger. Gabriel had noted on their first meeting that Pamela Milton was a woman who did not suffer fools gladly, but he suspected that there was quite a nasty temper lurking behind her calm exterior. "It was rather a long time ago, in case you have failed to notice," she answered tartly. "It did me no harm anyway. My parents were forced to give me a proper education in a decent establishment after that. One could say it was the making of me."

Gabriel smiled. "I'm very glad to hear it, Pamela, but that hardly answers my question. Why were you expelled?"

In her lap, Pamela's hands were shaking with what Gabriel suspected was suppressed rage. She stood up and walked to the door, throwing it open as though to see if Marion had arrived with tea, but no such reprieve had come. She turned back to face him. "I fail to see what this has to do with anything, but for your information I was expelled for, I quote, insulting those with whom I disagreed."

"Mrs Jennings, I presume?"

"The devil herself. I called her an ignorant old witch. Not without reason, I was thrown out posthaste."

"Why?"

Pamela looked flabbergasted. "Why do you think? For once, the old bag didn't have a choice! If she hadn't come down on me like a ton of bricks, she would never have exercised any authority again!"

"I meant, why did you say that?"

"Probably because she was an ignorant old witch, I suppose."

"Pamela . . ."

Pamela went very quiet. Her hands no longer shook; they were clenched together so tightly that the slender white bones showed beneath the taut flesh. She was employing every scrap of energy to avoid showing any weakness before Gabriel. "She called me a dirty Jew," she whispered. "Dirty little Jewess. She used to make me sit alone in the far corner of the classroom in an effort to protect the others. I don't even know how she knew about it. I have one Jewish grandfather, and he died years ago."

"I'm sorry," offered Gabriel gently. "Did you tell your parents what had happened?"

Pamela shook her head. "I didn't want to. I knew my father—God rest his soul—would have taken it very badly. His family had worked so hard to be accepted here all those years before. When his father arrived as a child, his parents even changed the family name to sound less foreign. Milton sounded so English, the name of one of the greatest English poets of all time. For all I know, she might simply have made an educated guess, but she had a tendency to find ways to hurt people." Pamela's eyes had closed with the effort of telling the story. "When I came home and told my parents I'd been expelled, of course they wanted to know why. I couldn't lie to them, and my father would never have given me a minute's peace until I had told him the truth." She paused to draw breath, her eyes still shut, but she sounded as though she had been running. "That was why I didn't get into trouble at home. My parents would never have accepted behaviour like that for any other reason. My father said I was to learn more sensible ways to express my disgust in future, but other than that, he left me alone." She glanced up at Gabriel with a sense of palpable relief. "A few weeks later, my trunk was packed, and I was on a train bound for the frozen north. It was a convent school. One of the sisters decided that I would be their first girl to go to Oxford, and Mother Mary Imelda was never wrong."

Gabriel paused, unwilling to draw the conversation away from Pamela's story, but the thought jumped out at him like a serpent. "Pamela, to your knowledge, was Mrs Jennings a Nazi sympathiser?"

Pamela shook her head again. "How would I know? We never spoke again, but I wouldn't put it past her. She was behaving like a Nazi before the Nazis had even come to power. And if she had been, she would have been intelligent enough to keep it to herself."

"Do you know anything about the bunker?"

Pamela looked at him as though he were an idiot. "Hitler's bunker? We all know about it. He topped himself down there."

"Pamela, I think you know what I mean."

Pamela looked disdainfully in his direction. Any former

emotion she had been suppressing had evaporated. "If I knew what you meant, Father, I should not have given you an answer you did not want."

They were interrupted by the sound of the door opening and the appearance of an agitated young woman armed with a tea tray. Scottie was bringing up the rear. "Awfully sorry, Madam," said Marion breathlessly, setting down the tray on the table between them. "Did you really mean me to serve Miss Charlotte's elevenses in the treehouse?"

"It's quite all right, Marion," answered Pamela apologetically. She rose to her feet to talk to the woman at eye level. "Charlotte can take her elevenses into the treehouse herself. She can use her thermos to avoid spillages."

Scottie was quietly sidling her way into the alcove in the bay window. Gabriel knew she was itching to join the conversation. "It's quite all right, Mummy," she put in sweetly. "I could just as easily eat in here with you."

Pamela chuckled. "Away outside! I'll call you from the window when it's time to come in."

Scottie sighed with theatrical hyperbole before stomping noisily out of the room with Marion. Gabriel was reminded of the frustration he had felt as a child, sitting on the landing and peering through the bannisters as his parents and their guests stood with their preprandial drinks, chattering about matters that felt very serious indeed and very important. It was not easy to be an inquisitive child on the fringes of an adult drama. "I shan't keep you much longer," said Gabriel as Pamela poured the tea. "I can't bear keeping you from that poor child any longer. I feel like a usurper."

Pamela laughed politely, but Scottie's sudden appearance had thrown her, and she struggled with the task of picking up the delicate milk jug and placing the silver sugar tongs within Gabriel's reach. The sugar bowl was bulging with neat white lumps, he noticed, and he doubted she had filched her supply entirely from George Smithson's cupboards. He made no comment as he helped himself.

"She gets far more attention than most children," Pamela remarked, "and I shan't be packing her off to boarding school either. I must say that I am thoroughly enjoying the task of educating her myself."

"She's a delightful child," said Gabriel, only partly to ingratiate himself with a woman he was about to risk angering again. "Pamela, if you'll forgive my asking, is George Smithson Scottie's father?"

Pamela started, never a good sign, and then burst into a fit of entirely forced laughter. "Dear me, no! He is very fond of her, and he indulges her because he knows it is an easy way to reach me, but no, no, no! I'm afraid he isn't. I wasn't lying when I said that Scottie's father died during the war. I'm sure he meant to make an honest woman of me when he returned, but fortunately for him, he was spared the horror."

The quip was in bad taste, but it had the desired effect, and Gabriel did not risk questioning her any further. He finished his tea as quickly as possible and took his leave.

13

How on earth did other detectives deal with their cases? Gabriel mused, as he dashed in the direction of the police station. The fact was that literary sleuths tended to be gentlemen with private means who had all the time in the world in which to indulge their curiosity. They could fight an intellectual battle for justice without having to worry about getting back in time for hearing confessions or training altar boys or comforting the dying. For that matter, how on earth had Father Brown managed it? A fine detective he certainly was, but what sort of a shirker of a priest must he have been? When had he ever had to bother himself with the minutiae of parish life, with the souls of tiresome, whingeing old ladies and fatherless children, and reforming gamblers and wife beaters? Perhaps the world had simply been a more ponderous place before continents had descended once again into the mire of a world war when millions were still bearing the wounds of the last one.

He was getting old and nostalgic, thought Gabriel despondently, further quickening his pace at the unimposing sight of the town constabulary as it emerged into view. It was not a view to strike fear into the heart of seasoned criminals or to evoke a sense of awed reassurance from law-abiding citizens. The police station was nestled into the middle of a long Victorian terrace, the familiar blue light hanging over the fifth door. Years ago, the *O* had fallen off or been stolen from the sign, making it look as though Gabriel were entering the residence of P LICE Esq.

He was still smiling at the thought as he arrived at the front desk and encountered the most fed-up-looking constable in the history of British policing. "Good morning, Stevens," greeted Gabriel, with hopeful cheerfulness. "How's little Marjorie feeling? Getting stronger, I hope?"

PC Stevens looked up from his work and gave Gabriel a half smile. "She's much better, Father. Thank you for asking. The doctor says she should make a full recovery."

"Thank God for that. You had a nasty scare."

Stevens nodded, allowing himself to be drawn fully into the conversation. "Aye, we had, and others were not so lucky. You heard about the Morgans, I suppose? They say little Tommy will never walk again. Why ever did God make polio, eh?"

Gabriel was about to proffer an answer when he became aware of heavy footsteps approaching him from behind, and he turned to face Inspector Applegate. "Not trying to ingratiate your way into my office by any chance, were you?" he asked wryly, turning to Stevens. "Watch out for this man. He will be wheedling information out of you before you know it. Or interfering with crime scenes, or tampering with evidence . . ."

Stevens and Gabriel began to answer at the same time. Then both stopped talking to allow the other man to speak. In the ensuing awkward silence, Gabriel said, "Inspector, I wonder if we might have a word?"

Applegate brushed past Gabriel in the direction of his

temporary office without making an answer. Gabriel suspected that the whole point was to belittle him into trotting behind him without any acknowledgement of his presence, but it was not the first time he had had to swallow his pride with Applegate. He followed him into the office. "As a matter of fact, I'm rather busy this morning," Applegate began, sitting at his desk in his coat. The room was very cold indeed, and Gabriel noticed a pair of hand-knitted fingerless gloves on Applegate's filing tray.

"Not busy spreading rumours about innocent men, were you?" asked Gabriel.

Applegate rolled his eyes. "All right, I overstepped the mark. I shouldn't have threatened you like that, but you really are a nuisance when you want to be."

"Consider it forgotten. What were you doing this morning then?"

"I was investigating a rather clever crime scene, since you ask."

"Yes, I know exactly where you were," answered Gabriel. He should have liked to have sat down, but Applegate did not offer him a chair, and he decided against riling the man by making himself too at home. "I told Douglas Jennings to inform you of the discovery. I asked George Smithson to take me down there last night as soon as I realised what had happened."

Applegate grimaced. "I suppose that's your way of telling me I owe you something, isn't it? What do you want?"

"I should like to take a look at the postmortem results, if you don't mind. Having seen the interior of the bunker, I'm fairly sure now how Enid Jennings died, but I should like to be certain."

Applegate smiled in spite of himself. He opened a drawer

and pulled out a brown cardboard folder, which looked as though it contained only a couple of sheets of paper and possibly some photographs of the body. "You know you've no business asking to look at this before I've had a chance to read it through myself, don't you?" Gabriel did not respond. "It's quite all right, Father. I knew perfectly well it was you who had worked it out. How about telling me how you found an invisible bunker if even I did not know about it? Then, perhaps you could tell me how you think Enid Jennings died. I'll take a look at the postmortem results, and we'll see if you're right."

Gabriel nodded. He knew that Applegate was deliberately patronising him, but it was the closest to cooperation he was going to get from the man, and he went along with it. "Very well, and if I'm right, you can buy me a pint."

"We'll see about that."

Gabriel gave up waiting to be invited to sit down and pulled up a chair, using the distraction to avoid thinking about the lives that would be ruined by the time the case closed. It was never just the guilty who suffered, and he was beginning to discover that sometimes even the guilty did not deserve to, but justice systems were not devised by people like him. "I believed that Agnes was telling the truth, and I could not accept that she was mad when there was simply no evidence to suggest it. That was really all there was to it. If she were telling the truth, then there had to be a rational explanation. Since there was absolutely no evidence in the area to back up her story, I concluded that the evidence must be hidden away somewhere very carefully. When Enid turned up dead where she did, I tried to ignore quite how far away she was found and simply thought of the nearest access to water, knowing that the river would have done the rest of the work itself. I know as well as you do that the war has left this country full of secrets—secret lives, hidden identities—so why not secret places too?"

"It was unwise to rumble George Smithson like that," suggested Applegate, determined not to offer Gabriel any encouragement whatsoever. "If he's guilty, he could find ways to disappear that even we can't get around. People like that tend to have—connections, shall we say?"

"If George Smithson is guilty, I suspect he is too clever to cut and run. His friends will protect him wherever he is," said Gabriel. He thought he would have to try to persuade Smithson to give himself up if it came to it, as there would be plenty of people to pull strings on his behalf and ensure that he was never arrested. That sort of invincibility made a man dangerous; it opened so many doors to temptation.

"Come along, Father, how did she die then?" prompted Applegate, throwing Gabriel's line of thought off-balance. Applegate had the file open and was trying unsuccessfully to hide his dissatisfaction with what he was reading. "Let's hear it from you."

Gabriel settled himself into his chair. "To start with, we may surmise that Enid Jennings knew her attacker. I think that has been clear from the start, but most victims know their attackers. Whoever abducted her—let's say 'abducted' for the moment—knew about the bunker, perhaps had always known about it. We are talking about an intelligent person who was capable of planning the perfect crime in tiny detail. This person—man or woman—entered the bunker from the opposite end, the river end, to avoid any chance of being seen in the vicinity of the house. The person then lay in wait by the open entrance, knowing that Enid Jennings would pass that way." Gabriel looked across at Applegate to see if the inspector was still listening. "But something was happening to Enid Jennings that her attacker had not anticipated. Agnes mentioned almost in passing that her mother seemed to be walking rather more slowly than usual. It is my belief, having observed Fr Foley recovering from a heart attack, that at the moment she was abducted, Mrs Jennings was already dying. As she walked along that path, she was suffering a heart attack, which left her out of breath and weak. It would have been even more straightforward than the attacker could have hoped to pull her through the hole, down the steps and into the main chamber."

"Father, the entrance would have been—"

"I'm coming to that, Inspector. I found her penknife partially opened on the floor of the bunker, and I couldn't help thinking it would be quite difficult for a woman to rummage in her handbag, take this thing out, and even partially open it, especially if she were feeling very unwell, very frightened and searching for it in virtual darkness. I don't imagine the assailant would have risked trying to get the lights on or pointed his torch in Mrs Jennings' direction to make things easier for her. It suggested to me that the attacker was sufficiently confident and clearheaded, that he quickly mounted the stairs and covered over the entrance before returning to her. If he knew what he was doing, it would have taken under a minute, but it would have been long enough for Mrs Jennings to get the knife out."

"But not quite long enough, since there's no evidence she actually used it. Her attacker reached her before she got the weapon open. Not that it would have been of much use to stab anyone, I suspect."

"The attacker did not stop her. Her heart did," Gabriel ventured. "A severe heart attack can kill a person almost instantly. In her case, she was given a few minutes. The shock of being snatched like that may well have finished her off. Let's face it, even a healthy person might faint if something so frightening happened to him. The would-be killer was spared the horror of committing murder but was left with a dead body. It could have been left where it was, but that had never been the plan, and our killer is a person who likes everything to tie up nicely. The killer had meant to force Mrs Jennings to walk the length of the bunker and drown her at the other end. It was obviously important that she not be found anywhere near her home to keep suspicion away from the family."

"Was it a member of the family?"

Gabriel ignored him. He had not finished answering his first question yet. "Unfortunately, very clever people do sometimes commit the stupidity of refusing to change their plans. It might well have been safer simply to leave the body where it was and hope that nobody would enter the bunker, or to take the body back out into the open and hope that when it was found, the assumption would be that she had collapsed as she walked home, but the attacker may well have felt it was already too late for that or feared that he might have been seen. So, the body was dragged the length of the bunker and dumped into the river, where any evidence could be washed away and it might even look as though she had drowned accidentally."

Applegate was staring piercingly at Gabriel over the top of the file as though Gabriel had personally choreographed the entire plan himself with the precise intention of annoying the police. "Well," he said after a judicious pause, "I can't vouch for your suppositions, but it says here that Enid Jennings did indeed die of a heart attack. She had no medical history of heart problems, but at her age, I suppose, anyone can suffer a heart attack. She did not drown, and there is no evidence of any injuries to suggest she met a violent end. The only suspicious observations are—"

"The grazed heel," interrupted Gabriel. "Yes, that would be consistent with the idea that she was dragged along the floor. I suspect you will find a shoe somewhere along that passageway. We didn't go all the way down—"

"You have viewed the body?"

"Yes. And the residual dirt under the fingernails, I thought that was a little odd when she was otherwise very well groomed. Well, I suspect she probably clawed the ground as she was dragged down the hole. There would have been a lot more dirt under her fingernails, but the river—"

Applegate threw down the file, stopping Gabriel in his tracks. "If you had already inveigled your way into the mortuary, why on earth did you need to see the postmortem results at all?"

"Well, I'm hardly an expert. I wanted to see the official findings. Why are you looking at me like that?"

Applegate had a nasty habit during interviews of standing up and leaning across the desk with his two fists bearing much of his weight, the intention being to intimidate the suspect sitting in the chair opposite him without actually touching him. Gabriel could have been convinced for a moment, with Applegate bearing down on him, that he was a suspect and was only minutes away from being charged. "Get out of my office," was all Applegate had to say to him, enunciating each word in a slow staccato. "You have led me to the crime scene. I have told you what you wanted. I think we're quits."

It was impossible for Gabriel to stand up without risking bumping heads with Applegate; he stretched out one hand to indicate that he wanted Applegate to step back, which he did as slowly and grudgingly as humanly possible. "Inspector, I merely accompanied Dr Whitehead to identify the body. I touched nothing; I interfered with nothing. I fail to see why—"

Applegate dropped back into his chair with a groan of frustration. "Look here, Father, it makes no difference either way. Since it looks quite clear that we are no longer dealing with a murder investigation, I am likely to be taken off the case altogether. My guess is that we are now looking at a kidnap charge, possibly with failure to allow proper burial of a body. It's unlikely we could even press a charge of manslaughter if she was already in the process of stuffing it when she was snatched, though that is not for me to decide. Whatever sort of crime this is, however, it is no longer murder."

"Isn't that a good thing?" asked Gabriel, staggering to his feet. "I feel quite relieved that there is no one in our vicinity with that crime on her conscience. Even if she had already committed murder in her heart, I suppose."

"She?"

Gabriel shook his head, making for the door. "Don't read too much into it. I get these feelings sometimes." He hesitated: "You must sense it every so often, Inspector, that feeling that the most important detail is not what one can see but what one cannot see."

Applegate shook his head impatiently. "Unless the person is missing, then no, Father, I'm afraid that's where we part company. What are you talking about?"

"I mean the body. If a person were abducted like that, the person who snatched her would have had good reason to believe that she would resist, even if not immediately. The attacker, of course, did not realise that Mrs Jennings was ill and unlikely to put up much of a struggle, but there were no cuts and grazes on the body to suggest rough handling. When Agnes was snatched, years ago—"

"What?"

"Sorry, Inspector, you don't know about that yet, do you?" asked Gabriel. "You'll have to ask Agnes. But you see, she was only a child, not capable of much resistance either, but her arms were marked from being held. The man who dragged her away held on to her tightly enough to be absolutely sure she could not escape."

Applegate held up a hand as though directing the traffic. "I wonder if we could pause a moment. Are you telling me that Agnes Jennings was also *abducted*? Years ago?"

"Yes," answered Gabriel absently. He rattled the door handle, but he appeared to be locked in. "Oh dear, I'm not sure I was supposed to pass that on to you. Oh well, never mind—anyway, what I meant was that whoever snatched Enid Jennings acted quite gently by comparison. Almost as though the abductor really didn't want to hurt her."

"The abductor was going to kill her, Father."

"But there was some impulse there, some instinct that stopped the person from hurting her. It would not have been easy to drag a grown woman down those steps without grazing or hurting her at all. I suppose that's why I keep thinking of a woman, though I daresay I may be being naive."

"You're being shamelessly naive, Father," Applegate agreed, moving purposefully towards the door with the key. "The most vicious attack I have ever received when arresting a suspect came from a woman who scratched my face like a wildcat, kneed me in the short and painfuls and attempted to remove my right ear. There never was such a thing as the gentle sex, I can assure you. Frankly, from the rumours I've heard about Enid Jennings, the victim herself rather proved that point."

~

Gabriel walked back to the presbytery with the feeling of having lost a vital match point against Applegate. That Mrs Jennings had been capable of serious violence was hardly news to him and was probably not news to any child who had ever entered her classroom, but a troubling thought ran through his head as he walked past the row of cottages, pausing at the cemetery gate to make the Sign of the Cross. Was it really the apparent gentleness of the abduction that made him think the attacker was a woman? It was only when Applegate had described that attack on his person that the thought had occurred to Gabriel: Enid Jennings' violence seemed to have been directed solely at other females, principally younger ones. Douglas had told him that his mother

197

had never once struck him, not *once*. He had clearly feared her, and he had witnessed some impressive scenes of rage, such as when he had attempted to hide his father's things, but that was not quite the same. The thought had barely registered with Gabriel at the time. Douglas was older than Agnes, and Gabriel had assumed that any discipline he had experienced in the house would have come from his father. *Mrs Jennings hated other women*, he thought. It was hardly an unusual situation, sadly, but hatred had a nasty tendency to become reciprocal. Agnes, Pamela—Therese perhaps?—there must have been others who might have been driven to return hate with hate or violence with violence. Pamela was so obviously not revealing everything she knew—could he really believe that Mrs Jennings had sent Pamela packing without harming or humiliating her at all? Would she really have been satisfied simply by expelling her?

Gabriel gazed through the bars of the graveyard at the rows of tombstones, glistening with the first frost in a way he would have thought magical as a child. At the far end, he could see old Mr Blewett praying at his wife's grave, the way he did every Friday without fail. She had died of influenza five years before, during the miserable December of '42, and Mr Blewett had admitted to Gabriel once that he still laid out her place for dinner every evening. In spite of his weekly visits to her grave, he still liked to think that it might all be an unfortunate mistake and she would walk into the dining room at seven o'clock one evening to take up her place at the table. He said it was sheer force of habit that made him check that there was a clean handkerchief under her pillow when he retired at night because she had a tendency to wake up sneezing, thanks perhaps to being a little sensitive to the down.

It struck Gabriel as he glanced at the frost-dusted flowers on Mrs Olson's grave that he could ask Mr Blewett the identity of the anonymous well-wisher, since their visits to the cemetery might have coincided. It was strange to need to know, but somehow Gabriel wanted to thank the man or woman for the thoughtfulness, that little reminder that even the loneliest souls are never forgotten. He waited until Mr Blewett had finished his devotions and waved in his direction. Mr Blewett waved back before moving towards Gabriel. "Good day, Father!"

"Good morning, Mr Blewett. Isn't it cold?"

"Cold enough for snow, I'll warrant." Mr Blewett was freezing, thought Gabriel. His coat was looking threadbare in places, and his fingertips protruded through the many holes in his gloves; there was no one at home now to knit him a new pair to see him through the winter. Gabriel made a mental note to ask Mrs Whitehead if she could knit him a pair for Christmas. "Mr Blewett, I wonder if you know who placed those flowers on Mrs Olson's grave? I was curious."

Mr Blewett looked where Gabriel was pointing. "Never noticed, I'm afraid. I'm always a little lost in my own thoughts these days." He stared back at the grave. "You know, I've not seen flowers there often. Whoever placed them there has only recently taken the trouble. Shall I keep an eye out?"

"No need to go to any trouble," said Gabriel, "but if you do happen to see the person again, I should like to know who it is."

Mr Blewett gave a mock salute. "Right you are, Father, I shall keep my eyes peeled."

With that, the two men parted company.

A few minutes later, Gabriel had more pressing concerns on his mind. He could hear voices upstairs as he walked into the presbytery and noticed a visitor's hat and coat hanging on the stand. He was about to race up the stairs when Dr Whitehead appeared on the landing and began to walk down towards him. "What's happened?" demanded Gabriel, his heart in his mouth. "Has he had another turn?"

Dr Whitehead gave the smile he had no doubt given to thousands of frightened friends and relatives over the years. "Calm yourself, Father. Just a routine appointment. I should have come yesterday to see how Fr Foley was getting on, but I'm afraid I became very behind. I didn't want to turn up too late in the evening when he might be resting." He raised an eyebrow at the sight of Gabriel's anxious expression. "Dear me, is this a guilty conscience?"

"I nearly had a heart attack myself, Doctor!" Gabriel leant against the wall to steady himself. "I'd forgotten he was due a going-over. I suppose you could call it a guilty conscience. I fear I have been a little negligent."

Dr Whitehead helped Gabriel into the kitchen and stood to attention as he settled into a chair. "Nothing to reproach yourself with, Father," he reassured him. "I'm glad to say he's doing very well. The company must be keeping his spirits up. I always find that is half the battle when a patient is convalescing from a long illness. Particularly when a man lives alone."

"Thank you." Gabriel contemplated asking the doctor

precisely how long it would be before Fr Foley made a full recovery and he could leave, but he could not think of a way of asking that would not sound churlish under the circumstances. "Might I offer you a cup of tea before you go? There was something I wanted to ask you if you're not in too much of a hurry."

Dr Whitehead shuffled his feet. Gabriel knew perfectly well that the doctor had many demands on his time, and any time he spent sitting in this kitchen would mean less time with people who really needed him, but he could not think of anyone else who could answer the question. "Well . . . how about a quick glass of water? Don't get up, I'll fetch it myself."

"Thank you. I shan't keep you; I know how busy you are." He watched Dr Whitehead fetching a glass from the correct cupboard. He knew where to find glasses from having poured water for Fr Foley before, no doubt, but his profession must have made him feel at home virtually everywhere. Gabriel also knew that Dr Whitehead was not likely to be remotely thirsty but was doing what he himself would have done when trying to put a person at ease. He was creating a homely distraction. "You remember when we went to view Mrs Jennings' body—God rest her soul—and realised she hadn't drowned? Well, I've just seen the postmortem results, and it's true. She did not drown at all; she died of a heart attack."

Dr Whitehead turned slowly to look at him. "Heart attack? That's strange, I don't recall . . . Well, I suppose with a woman that age it is quite possible. Am I to understand then that she was not in fact murdered?"

"Precisely. Someone evidently intended to murder her, but it looks as though God took her before someone else could do it."

"How extraordinary! Do you know something? It's almost a relief."

"That's exactly how I felt. I'm not sure the inspector understood what I meant."

"Oh no, it's infinitely better to think that no one did such a thing. Just a moment." Dr Whitehead paused a moment to fill a second glass with water. "But she was found floating in the river. If she didn't drown and she wasn't murdered, what was she doing there?"

"That was what I wanted to ask you," said Gabriel, taking the glass the doctor handed him. "The police think they know how she ended up in the river, but I have a medical question for you, if that's all right? You see, I'm not very familiar with heart attacks apart from what I have observed in Fr Foley, and he survived his. I have some idea that one's heart packs up, but nothing much else."

"That's more or less what happens, Father."

"Yes, but if Enid Jennings suffered a heart attack, does it mean she had a heart problem she was unaware of perhaps? Or can a sudden shock just kill a person like that, even a healthy person?"

Dr Whitehead brought his glass of water to the table and sat down. "It's rather like asking me why people die at all. She may have had a condition and failed to realise it. She may have dismissed the symptoms—the tiredness, the breathlessness—as merely old age creeping up on her, I suppose, but a serious shock can cause a heart attack in fairly fit people. If she fell or was pushed into freezing cold water, it certainly may have been enough to kill her. I knew a young man who died that way years ago. He was on his way home from a party; you know the sort of situation. It was dark, and he was rather drunk, lost his bearings. All alone with no one to fish him out, he would have passed out very quickly."

"I think Enid Jennings was dead before she reached the river," said Gabriel. "Could any serious shock have caused it?"

Dr Whitehead tried to hide his surprise. "I'd rather assumed you were talking about her falling into the river. Why do you suppose she died beforehand?" He shook his head as though to dismiss the idea. "Well, don't worry about that now. In answer to your question, yes, a serious shock could kill a person, but I think it more likely that a shock would be a contributing factor in a woman Enid Jennings' age. As far as I was aware, she was as fit and healthy as anyone, though she was not the sort of woman who would have troubled a doctor unless she were frothing at the mouth. My suspicion is that she had a weak heart to start with. A shock might have triggered a heart attack, but the heart attack may have simply happened."

"But Enid Jennings was not such a great age. With children the ages of Douglas and Agnes, was she even fifty?"

Dr Whitehead smiled sadly. "She married very late in the day, Father, but poor Enid was the sort of woman who was born old. Then, when her husband died, she aged overnight. Her hair went white. Perhaps it did take more of a strain on her health than she realised." He got up and took his glass over to the sink, where he quickly rinsed it out. "I'm afraid I need to clear off now. I have three more visits to make before afternoon surgery, and at least one of my patients could talk for England." He shook his hands dry and turned back to Gabriel. "Don't trouble yourself; I'll see myself out."

Gabriel got up out of habit and followed Dr Whitehead to the hall, watching as he prepared himself to leave. "How's Agnes?" he asked.

"Very much better, thank God." He glanced up from the task of buttoning his coat. "I meant to tell you actually: she's coming back to stay with us for a few days. Douglas told me first thing this morning that he doesn't think the police will trouble her any further, and he was going to get her out of Greenford's."

"That's excellent news . . ." Gabriel began, but he was distracted by a small white envelope on the doormat that he had either failed to notice as he walked in or that had only recently appeared. He bent down to pick it up. "Excuse me."

"There's nothing wrong with Greenford's; don't misunderstand me. It's a perfectly decent place . . ."

Gabriel was busy opening the envelope, having failed to recognise the handwriting on the front. "Indeed, indeed," he said, pulling out a small lined note folded once. "I daresay she will be more comfortable with you."

"Quite. It will be for only a few days, I suspect. Now that she is starting to get over the shock and knows that no one thinks she did it, she should hopefully start to settle down quite quickly."

Gabriel looked at the note. A short message, typed in block capitals read:

LEAVE PAMELA MILTON ALONE. I WILL NOT ASK YOU NICELY NEXT TIME.

"Indeed," answered Gabriel, but he could feel his heart thudding against his ribs, and it was not fear. "Do pass on my regards when you see her, Doctor. I'll try to visit her in the next day or two."

"Is anything the matter?" enquired Dr Whitehead, glancing from the note, which Gabriel had rapidly folded up, to Gabriel's livid face. "I do hope it's not an angry atheist."

Gabriel came to himself. "What? No, no, not all. Anyway, thank you for coming."

He waited as Dr Whitehead walked out of sight before he closed the door behind him, the note half crumpled in his hand. As he had already suggested to at least one of his suspects, a highly intelligent person could always be relied upon to do something exceptionally stupid at least once. The cleverest crimes were committed by idiots.

14

The bookshop was packed with customers when Gabriel entered, men and women searching for Christmas presents or ways of escape, but George looked towards the door as soon as he heard the bell. His reaction could not have been more instructive—a frozen smile that quickly thawed into a frown and a lowering of eyelids. "Good afternoon, Father," he said, with mock geniality, "and how may I help you this time?"

Gabriel walked up to the counter, removing his hat with an equally false gesture of courtesy. "I wondered whether you had a copy of *The Song of Bernadette*? Can't remember the author's name; it was unusual. Foreign. A neighbour recommended it."

"Sold my last copy this morning, I'm afraid, but I'll have more next week. I'll set one aside for you if you like."

"Thank you. That would be most kind."

"You'll be glad to know it's selling rather well."

"That is very pleasing."

George hesitated, running short of innocuous business talk. "Was there anything else?"

"I wonder if I could return a text I was sent in error. An epistle."

George grunted audibly, too sanguine to make a pretence at ignorance, and pointed Gabriel in the direction of the back room. "Sorry about that, old chap," he said. "Can't think how that can have happened. Let's see if we can sort it out, shall we?"

As soon as they were alone, George turned on Gabriel, hissing in a stage whisper. "Whatever you say, keep your voice down! One can hear everything out there."

"I think you know precisely what I am going to say," whispered Gabriel, matching his adversary's indignant tone. "That was the clumsiest attempt at a threat I have ever seen!"

George snatched the letter from Gabriel's hand. "Anyone could have written this," he protested, still whispering. He pulled out the piece of paper. "It's typed. Unless you've tested every typewriter in the town for a match?"

"The address rather gave it away. It's handwritten."

George looked askance at the envelope. "You couldn't possibly know if this is my handwriting," he said, a shade louder than before so that he sounded as though he were recovering from a heavy cold.

"Only a man as pedantic as you could have written out the address when you knew the letter would be hand delivered," said Gabriel, without making any further effort to whisper. "And it was written by a man who is used to writing in another language. The number seven is crossed. Not really the English style."

George studied the envelope just long enough to take in his mistake before throwing himself into the rocking chair. Gabriel had to hand it to the man that he was not the sort to waste time trying to save face. "She was very upset after you spoke with her," said George in an apologetic tone. "Raking over her childhood, asking personal questions about Scottie. You'd no right to do that to her. And of course I am not the father. What were you thinking?"

"I know."

"I do not have that honour."

Gabriel pulled out the stool and sat opposite George, regarding his bowed head very carefully before responding. "Mr Smithson, I hope you'll forgive my stating the obvious, but when a man trained as you have been acts so irrationally, it suggests only one thing."

George brought his face as close to Gabriel's as was decent to ensure that no one in the shop could possibly overhear. "I demand that you stop interfering, Father. If Pamela finds out about Agnes, she will never trust me again."

"You do not know that," answered Gabriel quietly. "She's hardly a sentimental little fool. If you'd only put two and two together, you'd realise that she too has a secret."

"What is that supposed to mean? What are you talking about?"

"Tell her the truth about Agnes and ask her to tell you the truth about Scottie. Then tell her how you really feel about her before some other chap does." Gabriel sprang to his feet and made a few quick steps to the connecting door, beyond which safety and company beckoned. "If it helps, you would be very well matched. You are both intelligent, educated, fiercely independent. And you are both far too young to be quite so trapped in your own pasts."

George stood up wearily. "You are a very clever man, Father, but you know nothing of what it means to love a woman."

Gabriel smiled, but he had to swallow hard before answering. "I too have a past, but I took my leave of it a long time ago." He took a deep breath like an athlete steadying himself before the starting pistol fires. "Now I think I had better offer my apologies to Dr Milton for the distress I have caused her."

Gabriel retreated from the room, glancing back to see George Smithson standing in silence, head bowed, as though he were a mourner at a graveside. The man's posture fitted Gabriel's mood exactly.

He knew he had unsettled Pamela by reminding her of a childhood experience that had changed the course of her life—for better or for worse, it would still have hurt abominably at the time—and things were about to get a great deal worse for her. Gabriel had that sensation he suspected women must have when they are unravelling a knot in a piece of handiwork and a long row of careful stitches starts coming apart, one stitch after another, until the whole work is in ruins. It had been the sight of Scottie cheerfully waving goodbye to him as he had left Pamela's house that had confirmed his belief that children lay at the heart of all of this; not only Agnes but other children conceived in war, the ones like Scottie who were confident of their place in the world and the others the world could not hold.

~

"I owe you an apology," Gabriel began, looking away from Pamela's stony expression. He was standing on her doorstep with Pamela showing no inclination whatsoever to let him in. "I had no business questioning you about your daughter in such a high-handed manner."

Pamela nodded pertly. "That's quite all right, Father, no offence." She clearly expected Gabriel to walk away, but he stood where he was. "Look here, Father, I hope you shan't think it rude if I do not let you in. It's just that my mother has taken Scottie out for the day so that I can get down to some writing, and I should rather not waste the time. I'm afraid my mother neglected to lock the gate as she left."

"I shan't waste your time," Gabriel assured her, "and you are not obliged to let me in. We can just as easily speak out here if you prefer."

Pamela glared coldly at him but could not quite bring herself to slam the door in his face. "Why are you doing this, Father? Why can't you just let well enough alone? You've upset Douglas and Agnes when they are both grieving, you've inconvenienced George—Mr Smithson. What business of yours is any of this?"

Gabriel took a step back, the way a tall man does to avoid appearing threatening. Not that he suspected Pamela capable of feeling threatened by any man. "Each man's death diminishes me," he said. "A woman has died in mysterious circumstances, and it seems only fair that the truth be permitted to emerge."

"Don't quote Donne at me, Father! I've never liked him very much—though it's practically heresy to admit it in my field. It's nonsense anyway; her death diminishes no one."

"Is that why you did it then? Because you believed her life to be worthless?"

Pamela's eyes blazed. With the instinct of a man who has seen combat, Gabriel caught hold of Pamela's raised hand to protect himself. "Give me one good reason why I shouldn't thump you right now!" she shouted.

Gabriel did not flinch, nor did he let go of her. "I can't help thinking a slap in the face would be more ladylike," he commented, "but I shouldn't do that either if I were you, Pamela. That would be one sin from which I cannot absolve you."

He felt Pamela's arm relax a second before she lowered her head, indicating to him that the moment of danger had passed. He let her go. "What is that supposed to mean?" she whispered.

"I mean," he answered softly, "that you have been living a lie and you have lied to me, with the best possible intentions. Now, why don't we both retreat from the cold and talk things over?"

Pamela nodded without looking at him and led him inside. Marion appeared in the hall at the sound of the front door closing. "It's quite all right, Marion," said Pamela with considerable composure. "I shall attend to Father. Please, could you ensure that we are not disturbed?"

Gabriel busied himself with the task of hanging up his coat and hat to allow Pamela time to step into the drawing room and collect herself. When he followed her and closed the door, she was seated by the fire waiting for him, her eyes shut as though she were praying. "Pamela," he began, seating himself opposite her. "Please do not ask for confession because you wish to tie my hands. If you have—"

"Father, I didn't kill her," she said tonelessly. "I didn't do it, though—God forgive me—I'd sooner put a medal than a noose around the neck of the person who did."

"Pamela, please don't"

"I had nothing to do with it, Father. Hear my confession and ask me under the seal, and I will give you the same answer. But I did want to kill her when I realised she knew about Scottie, though I have no idea how she can have worked it out. No one has ever *questioned* the situation. I was going to do it, Father. I couldn't bear her to hurt that child."

"Would you like to tell me what really happened?"

Pamela pulled a crisp linen handkerchief out of her pocket and scrunched it in her hand as though aware that she would need it. "Why do you need to hear it from me? You evidently know she's not mine."

"I guessed, that's all, and don't imagine anyone else will. She looks exactly like your child; the resemblance is striking. But there were things that struck me as a little odd, shall we say. If you'll forgive my being indelicate, you are clearly—well, *pure*."

Pamela blushed immediately. "How can you—*how*?" she blustered. "How can you possibly know a thing like that?"

"There you see, you blush very easily for a woman of the world," he answered, gently. "You blushed when I asked if George Smithson were Scottie's father, and it was not just because I had misunderstood the nature of your friendship. Then there's your relationship with Scottie herself."

"I'm a perfectly good mother," Pamela interrupted, the familiar terse tone breaking through her confusion. "She means everything to me."

"But of course. Don't misunderstand me. You truly are one of the most loving, most devoted mothers I have ever been honoured to meet. But there are times when the two of you look a little more like companions than mother and daughter, more the way I would expect a grown woman to treat a very much younger sister."

213

Pamela regarded him quietly. "Do you know something?" she asked finally. "You're like a child, Father. You suspect nothing and notice everything."

Gabriel pulled his purple stole out of his pocket. "Would you like me to hear your confession?" he asked. "You may find it easier this way."

Pamela nodded, but the sight of him draping the stole around his neck had the unfortunate effect of causing her to burst into tears. "Don't!" she begged. "Let me talk to you first. I swear I will tell you everything."

"Then why not make a clean breast of it, Pamela?"

"Because I'm not sure I am as sorry as I ought to be yet, and I know I will use the seal to stop you talking."

"Very well," answered Gabriel, folding the stole again and leaving it in his lap. "That's honest at least. Why don't you tell me what happened?"

"It's hard," she began, but she sounded so exhausted that Gabriel found himself straining to hear. "I have—I have lied to so many people, most importantly to an innocent child who had a right to know the truth. I am not her mother, but she believes that I am."

"Why?"

"Because I believed it was better for her to grow up thinking herself illegitimate than an orphan. I meant to tell her, truly; I was going to tell her when she was older. I was not lying when I said that her father died during the war. She is my brother Charlie's child, but you knew that."

"Well, it took very little deduction once I had realised she was not yours to assume she was the child of your twin. And it seemed reasonable that she might have been called

Charlotte in honour of a father called Charles, but also explained why you did not like her to be called Charlie. A little too close to the bone perhaps?"

"Yes."

"What can have possessed you to do this to her?"

"I'm afraid it all rather crept up on me, as lies so often do." She stared directly into the flames, ignoring the sight of Gabriel leaning silently towards her, scrutinising her every word. "Charlie married Bernie the year before the war broke out. Scottie was born two weeks after he left with his regiment for the Far East. He never saw her. They had moved back to Edinburgh to be closer to Bernie's family before it was publicly known that she was pregnant, but even her family were not able to help in the end. For months, none of us knew if Charlie were alive or dead, but eventually Bernie received a card from a fellow soldier, telling her he had died in captivity."

Gabriel's eyes were drawn to Charlie's photograph. "I'm so sorry, Pamela," he said, hating the lameness of it. He thought of the millions of families around the world who had received news like that, of the many wistful, monochrome faces staring down at loved ones in silent, undefined reproach. All those young dead faces . . . "I am so sorry, Pamela. I can't imagine what it must be like to lose a twin."

"It was harder for Bernie, and Scottie still so little. The poor thing was mad with grief, and no one knew how best to help her. I was still reeling from the news myself when I received a telegram from Bernie's parents telling me that she had thrown herself in front of a train. They were beside themselves, and there was this poor little mite without parents, and they were in no condition to care for her." Pamela turned to Gabriel imploringly. "It did not start out as a lie, you must believe me. I agreed to take care of her; that was all. I became her legal guardian. But of course, people talked. No one was prepared to believe that a young, unmarried woman would have adopted a child. We had the same surname, of course, and the resemblance was so strong that naturally people thought she was mine."

"So you decided to pretend that she was."

"Yes. It's absurd really; I would never have given my body to any man. I am fond of breaking the rules, but there are some lines I could never cross. If it hadn't all been so painful, the irony would have been glorious."

"Pamela . . ."

"Well it would!" she insisted, impatiently wiping away tears. "A friend of mine had to hide the bastard child she lost to keep up the pretence at respectability. I hid the fact that I had never been anywhere near a man, never given birth, even though it meant being denounced as a whore. Old biddies used to spit at me on my way out of church, and I used to hold my head high and laugh at them. I'm afraid I rather enjoyed being a rebel, Father."

"Evidently."

Pamela had rediscovered some of her customary energy in telling the story, and she looked sidelong at Gabriel. "Are you suitably disgusted, Father?"

"Not at all," answered Gabriel truthfully, without returning her glance, "but now that you have stopped lying to me, perhaps you had better stop lying to yourself."

"Father—"

"I do not believe for a single second that a woman of your considerable intellect and common sense would have given up her good name and lied so cruelly to a child simply to confirm the prejudices of nasty old gossips. I think this runs much deeper than that."

Pamela gave a vexed sigh. "I'm sorry, Father, but I have been honest with you when it gave me no pleasure to do so. What on earth are you driving at?"

"How did your brother die?"

"He died, Father," she answered, a little too hastily, but she seemed to know she was heading for a trap and had no intention of stepping into it. "That's all you need to know. Millions died; my brother had the misfortune to be one of them."

"Pamela . . ."

"Oh, don't 'Pamela' me! He died in a Jap POW camp. You must have some idea that he did not meet a peaceful end. Bernie's parents showed me the message. It simply said that he had died."

"You were his twin, Pamela. I don't imagine you required a message to tell you your brother had died. I suspect you already knew and perhaps had even worked out how he had died. Am I correct?"

Pamela looked fixedly into the fire, but even with her face pointing away from him, Gabriel could see that she was ashen. "Yes," she said dejectedly. "I knew he was dead. The peculiar thing was that I found out about his death shortly after being discharged from hospital. I was driving ambulances at the time, and one day I collapsed in agony. No explanation, no warning. I suddenly found myself on the

217

ground, writhing around with the most terrible stabbing pains I had ever experienced. They thought it was a burst appendix at first and rushed me to hospital, but it wasn't. The doctors came to the conclusion that it might be a weak heart. The pain was everywhere, you see, most severely in my chest. Of course, I knew it wasn't my heart, but how was I to tell the doctors I had felt my brother being murdered? It sounded too mad.''

"It's not unheard of, the connection between twins—" but Gabriel was silenced by the sight of Pamela's trembling shoulders. "I'm so sorry, my dear. I'm so sorry, but living your brother's life for him will never bring him back."

"One of the survivors told me what had happened!" Pamela burst out, but her voice cracked with the strain of speaking, and she battled with every word. "He told me he was in the camp—he was there with Charlie. He—he knew him. Charlie and some others tried to escape, but—well, there was nowhere for them to go. It was so—so stupid; they could never have reached safety!"

"Pamela, be careful," Gabriel interrupted, tapping the back of her hand as though to wake her up, but she was struggling to breathe, and he was afraid she might faint. "Calm yourself."

"When Charlie and the others were captured, they were tied to stakes in front of everyone—everyone—" She was speaking so quickly that the words tumbled into one another and were obscured even further by the sound of her gasps for breath. "The whole camp had to watch—then they were bayoneted to death. I can—I can still feel it— I can feel it sometimes. And Scottie is so like him. You've no idea; she's so very, very like him. His smile, even his mannerisms. When they asked me to care for her, I felt as though he had given her to me himself."

Gabriel sat in excruciating silence as Pamela rested her head on the arm of her chair and wept uncontrollably. He knew that there was nothing he could say that she would even hear in the state she was in, so he simply waited, resting his hand on her head as she drifted about in her own grief. She slowly began to quiet down. Her breathing became deeper and less laboured; Gabriel heard the telltale gulps and sobs as raw emotions were overcome by exhaustion. "It's all right, Pamela," he said, stepping back to allow her the space to sit up. "It's all right now."

"I'm sorry," she whispered, refusing to raise her head. "I'm sorry about all of it."

"It's all right, Pamela," he said, a little more firmly, "but I think you must listen to me now. You are an excellent mother to Scottie, and she loves you, but she has a right to know who she is. Telling her the truth will not make any difference to her feelings for you. She will always know you as her mother, and one day she will appreciate the sacrifices you have made for her."

Pamela slowly raised her head. Her face was so red and swollen that she was barely recognisable as the impish young woman he had watched commanding the attention of a lecture hall so recently. "Father, there were no sacrifices on my part at all," she said with absolute sincerity. "I am obsessed with memory; I have made it my life's work to study the way writers remember. Having a living embodiment of my brother's memory at my side could never be a sacrifice."

Gabriel was suddenly aware of a scuffle going on outside the door; then an ear-splitting thud as the door flew open and George Smithson stormed into the room, closely followed by a protesting Marion. "I don't care if she is not to be disturbed!" George snapped over his shoulder before staggering to a halt in the centre of the room. He stared at the pair of them. "What the devil's going on?"

"I'm sorry, Madam," Marion put in from the back of the room. "I told him not to come in. I thought Father was hearing your confession."

Gabriel stood up quickly. "It's quite all right, Marion. Dr Milton and I were just having a little chat. I'll be leaving now." He turned to Pamela, but George had already taken Gabriel's place by the fire and was holding Pamela resolutely by the hand. "Confession may have to wait for another day."

"Just a moment," George demanded to Gabriel's retreating back. "What's happened here? What have you done?"

"I came only to apologise," Gabriel began, turning around sheepishly.

"Well, you have made rather a dog's breakfast of that, haven't you?" answered George tartly. "Now I think you had better leave."

Gabriel smiled awkwardly and shuffled in the direction of the door, only to hear Pamela calling him to stop. "Father? Wait a moment." He turned to face her and noticed with some satisfaction that George had his arm around Pamela's shoulder. "Please don't tell a soul about this. I will tell Scottie. I think I should be the one to tell her."

Gabriel inclined his head. "Of course, Pamela. It is entirely right that you should. Now it seems to me that you two have a lot to tell one another." With that, he left the room, pausing in the hall just long enough to hear Pamela say to George, "I have something to tell you" and the response, "That's funny, me too." A moment later, Marion had closed the door and was helping Gabriel on with his coat. He hoped as he left that neither of them would realise he had set them both up to have this conversation, at least until after their secrets had emerged.

15

Gabriel took the long route from the Milton house to his next port of call, partly because he needed to straighten his thoughts but mostly because a yawning feeling of anxiety had taken hold of him again. No, it was not anxiety as such, though it felt a little like fear. He was feeling sad but also a sense of guilt that his sadness was misplaced in some way. A woman had died an unexpected death, frightened and alone, leaving this world in precisely the way Gabriel prayed every night that he would not leave it himself, and yet he felt so little pity for her. He knew that he had been remiss in failing to pray for her soul, but he had been overwhelmed from the start by the nagging apprehension that Enid Jennings had died with more wickedness to account for than he could know and that she had died without feeling a moment's remorse. But even if he had not known the full extent of Enid Jennings' crimes, someone who lived and breathed did know and had acted on the impulse to settle the score. Gabriel could never have explained this to Inspector Applegate, but he was desperate to find out the truth of what had happened on that lonely path and to meet the person responsible, because the culprit lived and might still be saved.

Gabriel became aware of an odd, uneven clip-clop growing louder, and he glanced up in confusion, half expecting to see a small lame donkey careering in his direction. Instead, a very red-faced, out-of-puff Mr Blewett limped frenetically in his direction, the metal caps of his old service boots tapping erratically on the paving stones as he hurried towards the priest. "Father!" he wheezed, snatching off his hat as he drew close enough. Mr Blewett came to a halt, panting like a marathon runner, his wiry, tweed-clad frame swaying alarmingly as he battled to catch his breath.

"My dear chap, what on earth is the matter?" demanded Gabriel, stepping towards him to take his arm. "What were you thinking, dashing about like that at your age? You'll give yourself a heart attack."

"I'm not a day over seventy!" wheezed Mr Blewett, using the sleeve of his jacket to wipe away the sweat that was gathering at his temples. "I saw you in the distance, and I had to catch you in time. I thought I was sure to be murdered if I forgot to pass on the information. Isn't that what always happens?"

"What?" Gabriel always battled to avoid an existential crisis during his conversations with members of the older generation, but this time he had no idea what the man was talking about. "Why would you be murdered?"

"Because I saw her! I saw the killer!"

Gabriel felt a small explosion of panic resonating through his chest. He looked round to see if anyone were within earshot, but they were alone. "What do you mean, Mr Blewett? Do you mean Mrs Jennings' killer?"

Mr Blewett nodded. "That was why you wanted to know who was leaving flowers at that grave, wasn't it? I thought as much as soon as you asked me. That priest is searching for a murderer, and he knows the killer is the one who leaves flowers. It's a signal. I read a Penny Dreadful once where a murderer did that."

"Mr Blewett—"

"He always left a bunch of irises at a tombstone in a deserted graveyard as a warning he was about to strike. There would be some significance in the choice of grave —a young woman who had died in childbirth, and so the victim would be a young mother; a five-year-old, and the next victim would be a little child—"

"No, no! You are quite mistaken!" Gabriel said emphatically. "I am so sorry, Mr Blewett. I'm afraid we were talking at cross purposes. I wanted to know who was being so kind as to lay flowers at Mrs Olson's grave because I wanted to thank the person. It has nothing to do with poor Mrs Jennings, God rest her soul."

Mr Blewett replaced his hat with an air of evident displeasure. "Well really, you might have said something. I very nearly confronted the lass meself."

"Lass?"

"Yes, pretty little thing. Surprised I didn't notice her before." Mr Blewett responded to Gabriel's frown with a satisfied smile, knowing he had given an answer the priest had not expected. "Now I think about it, she hardly looked like a Jack the Ripper."

"Who is she?"

"You know the girl I mean. Lots of blonde hair, goes about with a nipper in a pram. The doctor's daughter."

Gabriel sensed that Mr Blewett was watching his every move and endeavoured to smile. "Well now, isn't that kind?

A young woman busy with a little one still finds the time for an act of mercy. How kind!"

"Indeed. I shouldn't mind snuffing it meself if I had an angel like that praying for me. Good day to you, Father."

Gabriel waited until Mr Blewett had walked four or five yards before letting the smile slide off his face. *Oh Therese, what have you done?* he thought, forcing himself to put one foot in front of the other. He had not been lying when he had told Mr Blewett that the identity of the mysterious benefactor had nothing to do with Mrs Jennings. He had believed what he had said, or at least wanted to. Even in the midst of a nightmare such as a disappearance and death, a lonely grave is usually simply a lonely grave. It still was, just someone else's grave.

⁓

Gabriel arrived at the Whiteheads' house to find Agnes in the guest room, hurriedly packing her things. "Leaving so soon?" enquired Gabriel, causing Agnes to jump out of her skin. "It's quite all right. Mrs Gilbert told me you were leaving, and I thought I would catch you before you went."

"I'm sorry, Father, this really is not a convenient moment," she said breathlessly, throwing open the wardrobe with an air of near panic. "If it's about the funeral—"

"Yes, I was informed that the coroner had released the body. I was going to ask you about the arrangements."

"Not now, Father. Come and see me tomorrow at home."

"You are going home then? You've been back here only a day, surely?"

Agnes shook her head impatiently. "I've no business imposing any further. They've all been very kind, but I really should go home."

Gabriel closed the door softly. Agnes understood the gesture and threw down the armful of clothes she had been about to stuff into her suitcase. He was aware of just how young she looked; she might easily be a girl caught in the act of running away from school. "Agnes, it really is a little remiss of you to slip away when no one is around."

"I can't help that," she said, glancing anxiously at the closed door. "Dr Whitehead is out on his rounds, Mrs Whitehead is in the surgery, Therese—"

"Therese is doing a passable job of keeping herself and her baby away from you. But it's still not quite working, is it?"

Agnes looked at Gabriel in what might have been desperation. "I don't know what you mean, Father," she tried. "The baby's cries do rather get on my nerves, but I'm not used to it. That's all."

"Is that why they sent you to that clinic?" he asked gently. "You were in no fit state to go home then, but you couldn't bear being in the same house as a baby. And Therese knew perfectly well why."

Agnes hesitated as though weighing up how much he knew, then abruptly turned her back and continued the mad scramble to squeeze her personal possessions into her case. "Please go, Father. This is hardly the time."

Gabriel watched Agnes' hunched back as she worked, moving in short, nervous movements that reminded him of a small bird constantly searching for predators. "I am not

227

sure there has ever been a better time, since your baby is at the heart of all of this." Agnes spun round as though she had been slapped in the face. "Come now, Agnes, I realised when I saw you in church contemplating the Madonna and Child. You were not grieving for your lost mother at all, were you? You were grieving for your baby. Then I'm afraid a couple of people were rather indiscreet."

The colour drained from Agnes' already pale face, so dramatically that Gabriel dashed forward to grab her arm in case she fell. "Don't!" she snapped, with unexpected strength, brushing him off and pressing her hand against the wall to steady herself. Nevertheless, her knees buckled, and she slid slowly to the floor, sitting with her back to the wall as though she were in disgrace. "Virtually no one knew," she said quietly. "I told Pamela, and I think my mother told Douglas. No one was ever supposed to know."

Gabriel contemplated sitting down beside her, but she had made it perfectly clear she did not appreciate his presence, so he stood where he was. "You know you have nothing to be ashamed of, don't you?" he said.

Agnes stared glassily ahead of her. "My mother said I was a dirty little tart, bringing a bastard child into the world like that. But I don't remember a thing about it." She glanced up at Gabriel in what looked like anger. "I was blind drunk, Father! I don't remember having anything strong to drink at all that night—not a drop! But I must have, for a dare or something. *I can't remember.* All I know is that I woke up next morning in pain, with my clothing all over the place, and I had the most frightful headache."

"Agnes, this was not your fault. If some idiot got you

drunk, laced your cordial with something you wouldn't recognise, it was his fault, not yours."

Agnes appeared not to hear. "Well, the baby died. I suppose you know that too, but my mother said it was better that way. I would have had to give her up in the end."

"Her?"

"I wasn't allowed to look. They took the baby away, but I asked afterwards and the doctor said it was a girl."

There was a long pause, which under any other circumstances Gabriel would have taken as the cue to leave, but he knew Agnes had more to say, whether she wished to or not. He watched as she stared past him, trying hard not to blink in case tears came. Finally, without turning to look at him, she said: "Leave my baby alone; she had nothing to do with this. She was the only one who was truly innocent."

"She certainly was. An innocent victim."

At the word "victim" Agnes looked up at Gabriel in alarm. "What on earth are you saying? The baby was never going to survive, Father. She was born far too early."

"You were very frightened of your mother, weren't you, Agnes?" Gabriel said gently. "Fear and hate so often go together, but you have misdirected me from the start."

"I wasn't lying, Father! I couldn't remember a thing about the bunker. I only remembered when I took that funny turn the next day."

"No, Agnes," said Gabriel, "You knew as soon as you ran out into the darkness searching for your mother that there was only one place she could possibly have gone. I'll wager that you went a little further and covered up any evidence that the entrance to the bunker had been disturbed. You are the only person who would have noticed the telltale signs because you spotted them years before."

Agnes had clutched her head and begun rocking to and fro, her back hitting the wall over and over again as though she were deliberately trying to knock the breath out of her body. "I kept telling myself it wasn't real!" she shouted. "It felt like something out of a mediaeval poem. As though she had been dragged down to hell or the earth had swallowed her up. One minute she was there, and then she was gone, but I knew she'd been there. I could smell the lavender water she always wore."

Gabriel bent down and placed a hand on Agnes' shoulder to stop her from moving. "Agnes, why did you not tell the truth about what you knew?"

Agnes pushed him away, but she remained stock still, pressing herself back against the wall. "Do you really need me to tell you? Because I knew I was going to die! I knew I'd be shot if I told the inspector about the bunker and hanged if I didn't because everyone would think I had killed her."

"You were less afraid to hang?"

"Yes!" Agnes faltered, suddenly aware that she was shouting. "It sounds mad, but it was the thought of that man creeping up on me in the middle of the night . . . If I were condemned to death by a judge, at least I would know it was coming."

Gabriel smiled at the chilling logic of what she had said. "I suppose it is preferable to know the time and place, though most people would find that terrifying." He stepped quietly towards the door, opened it and looked out onto the landing before stepping back inside and closing it again. He had not heard the front door open downstairs, but he needed to be sure Applegate was not skulking about again. "You've been very brave, Agnes. I'm sure you regretted blurting out in your panic that you had seen your mother vanish, but once you had told the truth, you were not prepared to lie and retract the story. It's a pity you have not chosen to be more honest about the identity of the person responsible."

"I have no idea who did it!" protested Agnes, looking fixedly at the floor. "I didn't see anyone else! I saw that the ground had been disturbed, that much is true, but I didn't see anyone else!"

Gabriel sat down on the floor opposite Agnes, but she refused to look at him. "I know how much she provoked you, Agnes. It wasn't just those terrible moments of violence— and there were very few of those. It was the daily grind of living under the authority of a woman like that. All those little humiliations and privations; never being allowed to be a normal child. Never being able to invite a friend for tea, never even having the freedom to choose which frock to wear in the morning. She took control of every tiny detail of your life. And you have always known who took it upon himself to rescue you, haven't you?"

Gabriel was aware of the door opening softly behind them and the firm, confident tread of Dr Whitehead entering the room. "Why don't you leave her alone, Father?" he asked softly. "Please. She has done nothing wrong."

"Protecting the guilty might be considered wrong, Doctor."

"Keeping her mouth shut hardly makes her an accomplice. I think you know that. Now why don't you leave the poor girl alone and come downstairs?"

Gabriel stood up slowly, hampered by the unpleasant

sensation of pins and needles in his feet. He was getting too old to sit cross-legged on bare floorboards. "Let's have a nice cup of tea," he suggested, turning back to nod at Agnes. "I must apologise for distressing you, my dear. Let me leave you to pack."

Gabriel followed Dr Whitehead downstairs in absolute silence, noticing only how slowly the doctor was walking and how unlike him it was to have drooped shoulders. It was only when they stepped into the kitchen, where Mrs Whitehead and Therese were sitting and waiting for him, that he noticed how pale and tired they all looked. The kettle whistled suddenly, causing the three of them to flinch, but Mrs Whitehead turned to the stove in what was almost relief, occupying herself with the task of pouring the boiling water into a large old teapot. The kitchen did not look quite so homely and safe this morning, but Gabriel put it down to the dismal day outside, which was making the room unusually dark.

"You knew it was me all along, didn't you?" asked Dr Whitehead, sitting down wearily at the table. He did not invite Gabriel to join them, but Gabriel preferred it that way.

"Not all along, no," Gabriel admitted, "though Agnes inadvertently gave me a clue quite early without realising it. She said that with a pair of binoculars it would be possible to see everything around. It put me in mind of a birdwatcher, a hobby I somehow associated with a man of a certain age. The floods would have receded unevenly in that area, making it easier to spot even a small undulation. That was when you noticed the bunker, wasn't it?"

"Yes. I'm afraid I have a boyish curiosity about such

things. I never intended to misuse it to begin with. I'm not quite sure where the idea came from."

"But when you told me about little Archie's disappearance, you were unwittingly confessing. As, of course, you were when you drew my attention to the fact that Enid did not drown."

Dr Whitehead looked miserably in the direction of his wife and daughter, who were both in tears. "Why don't you go?" he almost pleaded. "I should find it easier to talk to the priest without an audience, if you can bear it."

Therese placed a hand on his arm. "This is all my fault," she whispered. "You leave. Let me confess everything."

Gabriel watched as the doctor drew Therese into his arms. He was so much bigger than she that he was able to lift her into his lap as though she were still a child. For a moment, that was exactly what she looked like. She had tied her hair back with a blue ribbon that would not have looked out of place accompanying a gymslip. Gabriel felt the queasiness in the pit of his stomach again. Applegate would never have worked it out. He would never have brought such misery to a family. "I will not leave this house without hearing your confession," said Gabriel, though he was not sure how much Therese could hear, "though I am sure at the time you thought it a harmless prank to lace Agnes' drink with alcohol. It was you who got her drunk, wasn't it?"

Therese nodded without looking at him. "I can't even remember whose idea it was to mess around with her drink and set her up with a soldier, but I was the one who did it. I didn't stop and think how it would end, we were just larking about."

"And I dare say you left long before things turned nasty."

Therese whimpered into her father's shoulder, but it was Dr Whitehead who answered. "Therese has been tortured by the events of that night for years. I know that what she did was very, very wrong, but they were little more than children. It would never have occurred to her that the man would, well, do what he did."

Therese turned her streaming face in Gabriel's direction. "Agnes stopped speaking to me after that—she hardly spoke to anyone—but then—then when I found out months later that she was very ill, I knew what I'd done."

Dr Whitehead held Therese a little tighter, more to silence her, Gabriel suspected, than to offer comfort. "Therese told me everything. I knew Agnes would never have chosen to do anything that disgraceful. She was a complete innocent, never had a stiff drink in her life. Never had a boyfriend." He looked across the table at his wife. "Darling, please take Therese out of the room." The two women began to protest, but the doctor rose to his feet, forcing Therese to stand up and move away. She looked at him as though he were abandoning her. "There are some details I am not free to share. *Please.*"

Gabriel watched with ever-growing despair as Dr Whitehead walked with his family to the door as though seeing them off at a railway station. He reached out and squeezed his wife's hand for a moment, saying quietly, "It's all right. It's all going to be all right."

"You told them about Agnes' baby then," commented Gabriel, when they were alone.

"I had no choice, Father. I don't bandy patients' details about easily, I assure you."

"That's why you never told a soul how close you came to losing two innocent lives that night."

Dr Whitehead looked up sharply at Gabriel. "I had no idea what I was going to find when I entered that house. Enid had told me only that Agnes was unwell and in pain. Agnes had concealed her pregnancy from everyone, including her mother. Heaven knows how much longer she would have tried to hide it, but she went into premature labour and her mother heard her moaning."

"How far along was she?"

"Agnes was able to tell me that she was about twenty weeks. Her waters had broken, I knew there was no chance that the baby could survive." Dr Whitehead shook his head. "You have no idea how terrible it is when a patient pleads like that: 'Save my baby, Doctor! Please. Please save my baby! I'll do *anything* . . .' I'm afraid that there are some processes that cannot be stopped. I did all that I could do. I attended Agnes as she laboured and then delivered her baby, I cut the cord, wrapped the baby up in a towel and performed an emergency baptism. She died in my arms with poor Agnes still screaming at me to save her . . . All the while, Enid did nothing to help her daughter."

Gabriel regarded Dr Whitehead's bowed grey head. These moments of intense emotion always heightened his awareness, but all Gabriel noticed was the absolute, unnatural silence all around them. Therese's baby was asleep or had been taken out, and wherever the other women of the house were, they were deliberately keeping their distance. He could hear neither footsteps nor muffled voices in other rooms. "Doctor, however heartless Enid Jennings was that night, you were never her judge."

"Father, she very nearly had her daughter's life on her conscience." Dr Whitehead looked almost pleadingly at Gabriel. "You were right to guess that I nearly lost Agnes that night; I assume you worked it out based on her poor health now. Haemorrhage is a common complication following miscarriage or childbirth, but we doctors dread the sight of it more than anything else. There was no telephone at the house at the time, so I begged Enid to run for help. She was a fit woman and could have reached the nearest kiosk in good time."

"She refused?"

"Of course. I told her that Aggie would bleed to death if she didn't call an ambulance, but she wouldn't budge. I started shouting at her; I became desperate. She stood there, looking on as her daughter bled, without any concern at all that she might lose her."

"But you saved her."

"Yes. I did not dare leave Agnes alone, so I pushed Enid aside and carried Agnes all the way to my car, then drove her to the hospital myself. We only just made it in time, and Agnes has been in poor health ever since."

"I'm getting stronger, thanks to you," said a surprisingly bright voice from the doorway. Agnes was standing with her arms folded, leaning against the wooden doorframe in an almost casual manner. "I won't let him hang, Father. She didn't care about anyone's life after my father died. Why should hers matter now?"

Gabriel extended a hand to Agnes by way of invitation; she took the hint and joined them at the table, though the air of weary insolence hung about her like an odour. "I think you know what my answer to that would be, Aggie. But you should also know that no one will hang for this. There was no murder, was there, doctor? You hesitated when it came to it."

The doctor looked almost embarrassed. "It's no easy business ending a life, Father, especially for a doctor; murder was never my intention. I overheard Enid threatening Pamela after that lecture. I had seen how vindictive she was capable of being, and I knew she was capable of destroying Pamela if she chose to, perhaps Scottie too. They'd been through so much, I couldn't bear the thought of her hurting anyone else. I wanted to threaten her, threaten to expose her as the heartless monster she was if she wouldn't back down once and for all. I knew she was the sort of person who would only listen to reason if someone frightened the life out of her."

"Well, you certainly did that," Gabriel responded, a little more tersely than he had intended. "I'm not sure I know you well enough to be certain that you did not intend murder, Doctor, but if you did, you were spared the sin."

Doctor Whitehead nodded. "I did not mean to kill her, though I understand that you might find that difficult to believe under the circumstances. But without knowing it, Enid was dying as she walked towards her house. That was why she walked so slowly and paused to catch her breath."

"A heart attack."

"Yes."

"Why did you go through the hassle of dragging her body the length of that bunker? You might just as easily have left her where she was."

"I couldn't risk the bunker being discovered and the body being found so close to the house. Agnes or Douglas might have been blamed. But in the event, Agnes was blamed anyway."

"That was an unfortunate mistake, wasn't it? When you heard that Agnes and Pamela would be dining together you assumed that Agnes would be a guest at Pamela's table, since Enid hated Pamela. You assumed that there would be no one at the house that afternoon."

"Yes. I caught sight of the light in the window only as I reached up to snatch Enid, and by then it was too late. I moved as quickly as I could to ensure I was not seen, but of course Agnes had noticed Enid walking along the path."

Gabriel was distracted for a moment by Agnes lifting the teapot from the centre of the table. The distraction had the effect of breaking the tension between them. Even the doctor sat back and drew a long breath.

"Doctor, you should have confided in me," Agnes said. "It would have saved you so much trouble. You could have put her body back on the path, then I could have called for help and said I saw her collapse as she walked towards the house."

"I'm afraid I did not expect you to be so—" The doctor searched for an appropriate word.

"Heartless? No, I suppose you imagined I'd blame you and start shouting 'murderer!' all over the town."

"You know you would not have been as phlegmatic about it as you imagine," said Dr Whitehead. "It would have been a disaster if you'd seen what I'd done."

Agnes shrugged. "We could argue about that forever, but it's beside the point. No one needs to know. No one will ever guess. And if she just died, there's no crime, is there?"

"Kidnapping, dumping a body, interfering with a police

investigation," Gabriel ventured. "Probably not manslaughter if it can be proven beyond reasonable doubt that your mother was already in the process of suffering a fatal heart attack when she was snatched. Then there is the small matter of what you did to Mrs Olson's grave."

Dr Whitehead sat bolt upright. "She was a generous soul, Father, she would not have minded sharing her grave with a little one."

"Father, *please*." Agnes had taken hold of his hand, which Gabriel found almost unbearable.

"Aggie, it's quite all right," Dr Whitehead began. "Leave it now."

"No, I won't let you take responsibility for that," she said emphatically. "Father, I disposed of the baby myself."

"You can't possibly have done," answered Gabriel calmly. "Mrs Olson died all alone. Fr Foley told me that there was only one person at her Requiem—but if the woman was all alone, who would even know she had died? Apart from the person who signed her death certificate." Gabriel looked at Dr Whitehead. "If I am right, Doctor, when you returned to Enid the next day to report on Agnes, she presented you with a little bundle to dispose of. Am I right?"

Dr Whitehead looked anxiously at Agnes, but she had closed her eyes. "It was not like Enid to be squeamish, but she said she had been unable to bring herself to dispose of it herself." He glanced at Agnes again, but she was motionless. "I wanted to give the baby a decent burial, but Enid was determined that no one would know of the baby's existence. She said Agnes could never live with the shame."

"Not my shame," whispered Agnes, without moving. "No one asked me."

"So you went to Mrs Olson's Requiem the following morning," continued Gabriel, "and waited behind at the graveside until the gravediggers had finished their work."

"Yes. It felt horribly macabre to have to stand solemnly at the graveside knowing that I had that tiny baby hidden inside my jacket, but as soon as I was alone, I buried her in the upturned soil of the grave. The baby had a Christian burial of sorts."

The three of them sat in silence, each one unwilling to be the first to speak. Gabriel felt the urge to get up and switch on the light; the oppressive darkness of the room had become stifling. Eventually, he could bear it no longer, stood up and walked over to the switch. The sudden burst of light caused the other two to blink in surprise as though they had been buried alive for weeks. "That's better," he said, sitting back down. "Now we can see one another clearly."

"What will happen to Dr Whitehead if he confesses to the police?" asked Agnes. "What will happen to his family?"

"I am not a policeman," said Gabriel, "or a solicitor. Your brother would be better placed to advise on this. There will be a public trial, though there is an outside chance, Doctor, that you might escape prison if you have a good enough defence counsel."

"I'll be struck off," added Dr Whitehead. "I shall lose my reputation. In some ways, I think I'd sooner hang. Father, may I ask a question?"

"Of course."

"I know the truth should come out, but could it wait six months?"

"Why?"

"Because in six months I shall retire. If necessary, we can

move away and my family can start afresh, far from gossiping tongues."

"And Agnes will be far away," added Gabriel, looking in Agnes' direction. "Am I right?"

Agnes gave a startled smile. "Yes, as it happens. I planned to go abroad a long time ago, but I have not been well enough. I was trying to pluck up the courage to tell mother, but she died before I could. I'm going to India."

Gabriel looked at her in surprise. "But we've left India."

"I'm not going as a colonial, Father," she explained. "Those days are over. Pamela has found me a position at a new school in Bombay. A Catholic school. New school, new country. It seems a fine place to start a new life."

"Please, Father, please consider this," said Dr Whitehead. "If I had killed Enid Jennings, I would be prepared to account for her death immediately, even if it meant going to the gallows. I am not asking you to bury the truth, simply to postpone telling the police what you know."

Gabriel pondered the two expectant faces. He had not thought much beyond confronting Dr Whitehead with what he knew, and he hesitated now, shaken by an unexpected sense of uncertainty. "Applegate is no longer in charge of the case," said Gabriel slowly. "Once it was established that Enid Jennings was unlikely to have been murdered, the case was transferred to more junior hands. I think it unlikely that the police will ever work out what happened, more through indifference than anything else. The public expect a murder to be solved and punished. A case like this, whilst intriguing, is unlikely to be a priority for busy constables trying to keep the peace." He looked at Dr Whitehead. "Doctor, I want you to do something for me."

"Yes?" he asked warily.

"I want you to write me a confession. I want you to write a truthful account of your actions, including your motives for acting as you did. Sign it and seal it, then entrust it to me. In six months' time, I will hand over your confession to a policeman I trust. Your fate will then be in the hands of the law."

Dr Whitehead nodded resignedly. "Thank you."

Gabriel got up to leave. "There's something else I should say, Doctor. I have no doubt that you are a good man, and I for one am grateful that providence prevented you from committing such a crime, but I find it hard to believe that you only meant to frighten her. In your heart, you had already committed murder. Perhaps you should ask yourself how you came to hate another person—however wicked she was—to the point of being prepared to go to such lengths to end her life."

Dr Whitehead stepped past Gabriel as though to escort him to the front door. "Father, may I come to you for confession later today? I'll bring Therese with me."

Gabriel nodded. "Come this evening when you have had some time to think over things. I'll be expecting you."

"Thank you." He paused, glancing back to see if Agnes had followed them out of the kitchen, but she was not there. "I suppose, in answer to your question, it came down to justice. I have attended many patients who have been hurt by others, and it is hard not to feel quite overcome with rage at times, especially when it is clear that there will be no justice for them. If Enid had beaten a grown woman to within an inch of her life, she would have faced a lengthy prison sentence for grievous bodily harm, but Agnes was

242

only a child and nobody cared. When she did everything she could to stop me from saving her own daughter's life, her actions came perilously close to attempted murder, but even if Agnes had died, Enid would never have been punished. When I heard her threatening to destroy Pamela's life, I knew Enid could get away with that too, but this time I could stop her. So, I did. It was almost too easy."

"Not so easy," Gabriel put in, winding his long black scarf around his neck. He was aware of the hundreds of stitches Mrs Whitehead had knitted to make the thing and the hours she had expended on his behalf. "It was one of the most needlessly complicated, carefully planned crimes I have ever come across. There were so many opportunities to resist the temptation to carry it through."

"For what it's worth, I wish I hadn't done it," answered Dr Whitehead, frankly. "As soon as I had dragged her down those steps, I began to panic. I'm not sure precisely what I would have done if she had not obliged me by dying like that."

Gabriel opened the door and stepped onto the path outside. "Take some comfort from that then," he said.

"Thank you."

It was painfully cold, but Gabriel suspected the worst was yet to come. "I hope we are not heading for another terrible winter."

"I cannot say I am in any hurry for the summer to come, Father," answered Dr Whitehead from the shelter of the doorway. "I shall see you again this evening."

16

"So I shan't be getting rid of you just yet after all," said Fr Foley, reading the letter Gabriel had handed to him over dinner. "Well, I can't say I'm not a little relieved. I've grown rather used to the company."

Gabriel helped himself to the pile of potato cakes Dorothy had prepared for them. It was at times such as this that he tried to imagine what a steak looked like—a great big juicy rump steak covering his entire plate, replete with mushrooms and potatoes and carrots and peas. But mostly just the steak, oozing with blood to suit his one continental taste. "Excellent potato cakes," he said flatly. "Nicely seasoned."

"It's good of your abbot to spare you for another nine months. I expected that you would be called back to the abbey after Christmas."

"I asked permission to stay with you a little longer," Gabriel explained, "just to make sure you are entirely recovered. I'm starting to feel quite at home."

Gabriel returned Fr Foley's indulgent smile across the table and thought of Agnes, who was preparing to sail thousands of miles away to a new life far from everything she had ever known. He felt quite ashamed when he thought of the fear he had felt when he had made the decision to enter the religious life after his own life had taken an unexpected course. Such fear and trepidation, so many second thoughts, so many backward glances. But then, no new beginning was easy, wherever it occurred.

Gabriel slipped his hand into his pocket and let his fingertips brush over the velvet material of his purple keepsake bag. It was almost a genuflection to the past, but now it contained Dr Whitehead's letter, the cream envelope sealed with wax to make extra sure no one would open it in error. For the first time in his entire life, Gabriel was in no hurry for the summer to come either.